PUMPKIN SURPRISE

-POEM-

THOMAS L. LAIDLER

Published by Studio of Books

ISBN 978-1-964929-27-9 (paperback)
ISBN 978-1-964929-28-6 (digital)

Printed in the United States of America

THE CREW

These three best friends unto the end,
An alliance they did form.
Through weather thick and weather thin,
Nothing could sever their bond.

Now hear the tale of one such dread
That tried their courage true
To see if they would buckle in
Or stand as one tight crew.

Would they keep their loyalty deep
And hold on all the way
To brave the tide, whatever it brings
And no wise go astray?

With always a plan, Tonie the brain,
The smartest of them by far,
Would keep them on the narrow path
Lest they should miss their mark.

Yea, Ann, the cutest of them all,
Did have a fiery spark.
With dazzling eyes and shining hair,
She, too, did have some smart.

And then there's Tommie, the only male,
That balanced out the group.
As muscled bound as was polite,
Together, what couldn't they do?

By happen chance they were invited
To a party for Halloween.
Not one of them, not two of them,
But all three on the team.

A very unique, exclusive group,
Their solicitors were indeed.
It was all strange and so hush-hush.
'Twas quite hard to believe.

At length they so discussed their options
Of whether or not to go
Where they so gathered at Charlie's Lounge,
Their favorite place in tow.

Many discussions were on their plate.
'Twas the meeting of the minds.
Besides this too, they also wanted
To take the time to dine.

Tonie's mind was mainly set
On the comet of the night.
She wanted to be where she could see
This phenomenon on sight.
But Ann and Tommie did steer their course
Toward a different train of thought,
For their excitement was totally set
On the invitations brought.

"It'll be such fun to meet new guys,"
Said Ann with much delight.
And Tommie added, "There's other perks"
And privileges that do reside.

This party, it will be the bomb
That puts us on the map.
Joined with the elite, we're on our way.
No more will we take crap."

Reluctantly, Tonie finally caves in
And gives them her attention
As they discuss the invitations
With the comet mentioned.

"It's very strange that all of us
Acquired these invitations
As if we were especially chosen
And that on the same day.

Indeed, this may just be the case,
But when all's said and done,
We will at least have given our best.
And plus, we'll have some fun.
This special party will come but once
For us to take a ride,
To better ourselves, move up the ladder,
And make for better lives.

And if it all completely dives,
And turns out as a bust,
With all the food and entertainment,
There'll be no need to fuss."

With a final nod, they all agree
The party to attend,
And though they're hungry and starving now,
They'll put this off till then.

The Tale

Ann's now gone; Tommie turns to Tonie.
And this is what he says,
"I saw that look upon your face
As if you glimpsed the dead.

When we'd mentioned Professor Goofball
And the stories that he tells,
For one split second your face turned white
As if you'd looked in hell.

So level now and tell me straight
What is it that you know
To make you weary of Halloween
To this party we want to go?"

"Even though Professor Governberg
Is strange in his own way,
His facts indeed are very valid
If you listen to what he says.

Now listen close to what I heard
And keep an open mind
And tell me if you still intend
To stay in step with time.
A sister and brother of our same age,
It was sometime ago,
Who did attend our very own school,
Also received a note.

A special event they did attend,
Much like what we have now.
A full lit moon and strange set stars
Did lead them out of town.

For many a days they were lost,
Dead to the public view.
Then just as sudden, they reappeared
Without a hint or glue.

And they indeed were changed a lot,
Came out no more by day.
But rumors were, it was at night
That they went out to play.

Then all at once, it happened quick.
They all did disappear.
The entire family no more seen,
Now tell me that's not weird.

Yet everything that they possessed,
Their clothes, cars, house, stayed there.
Nothing disturbed from the biggest item
Down to the smallest ware.
Tommie paled but just a little,
Then righted himself right quick.
"Yo, Tonie, I say, yea, that was then,
And we're not in that mix.

Right now let us just get it together,
Enjoy the opportunity,
And make the most of Halloween
With both you, Ann, and me.

So with this settled, let's now go home
And thus prepare ourselves
And rendezvous at the appointed place,
Being sure that we're all there."

At Tonie's Place

Now, Tonie whined, "Do I have to?
Oh, Mom, I will be late
If I must stop at Aunt Tab's house
As I go on my way."

Her mother looks and eyes her hard,
And Tonie's stomach drops.
'Twas a very bad move defying her mother,
And now she's in a spot.

Now isolated in her own room,
Mom standing in the door,
She may have just lost all her points,
No Halloween galore.

She sees it clearly in Mom's eyes,
The doubt that threatens to rise
To keep her from the Halloween party,
A longing she desires.

Her mother calls unto the dad
While leaning out the door.
Her words are shrill and very high
And carrying great remorse.
"Oh, Harry dear." Her voice is heard
Out in the living room,
And as with Tonie, it targets him
To bring a note of gloom.

He knows this state of pending doom
When his wife makes this call.
He knows a tempest is on the way
And hopes there's no great fall.

Now Tonie begs with pleading eyes
And grasps her mother's hand,
Giving all she has in a warming voice,
Which is at her command.

"Oh, pretty please. Oh, Mommy dear.
I do recant my tone.
I meant no harm nor disrespect.
Don't make me now stay home."

With trembling limbs and wobbling knees,
There's nothing more to do
But hope and pray deep in her heart
That fortune will pull through.

The seconds tick like crawling hours
As Mom and daughter face off.
There's anticipation plus heartfelt grief
Until Mom's face goes soft.
Again her mother leans out the door
And signals to her Harry
That all is well, a false alarm,
All things again are merry.

Tonie hugs her mom with great relief
And smiles a silent prayer,
Thanking Mom for all she's done
And truly being right there.

But Mom forewarns her, telling her straight,
"Do not forget your charge,
For if you do, I will come back
And tan your bottom hard."

Needless to say, Tonie leaves the house,
Brimming and gleaming with joy,
That she is able to make the party
As she steps out the door.

At Tommie's Place

Meanwhile at her other friend's house,
Tommie stands aloft,
Before the mirror admiring himself
And lost in his own thoughts.

His chosen outfit suits him well,
Caught up in his attire,
His mind lost in a faraway place
And wooed by some strange vibe.

Now focusing on the invitation
That's on his tabletop,
He's unaware of his audience,
Who stands there on the spot.

So thus it is with mocked surprise
When brought back down to earth,
That upon him hearing his brother's voice,
He's filled with awe and mirth.

Oh wow! Oh wow! Just look at you,
You are the very bomb.
Even the man, Rambo himself,
Do not possess such charm.

Now startled back into reality,
Tommie first is filled with anger,
Next fear, confusion, then compassion,
Then something much, much stranger.

But when at last it comes together
And he sees his little brother,
That simple face with beaming eyes,
That other stuff his love smothers.

With confirmation of his costume
From his brother's thrilled reaction,
He's ready to go and get it on
And make this party happen.

Saying "So long" to Mom and family,
He heads on out the door;
And who should meet him on his lawn
But Tonie, no less no more.

Two out of three is not so bad
As they move down the road
To be acquainted very soon
With Ann to make them whole.

They talk of this and talk of that
To pass the time away.
They truly hope that Ann is ready
And do not make them late.
For Ann is known to prime and preen
To make sure all is right;
But this also would throw them off,
Which will not do tonight.

And finally they're at her house
And is about to knock.
When suddenly the door flies open,
And through it Ann pops out.

She is stunning, as well as dashing,
And what indeed a view.
There are no words to capture it all;
She is indeed a beauty.

THE WARNING BEGINS

With open mouths, excited stares,
Together they walk on,
Using the map with the invitations
Received in its own form.

The familiar path that they now take,
It leads them to the church,
Which straighten their hairs and prickle their skin,
As if to ward off hurt.

They look together and see the church
That shines as if a beacon,
Standing there in the midnight hour,
As if to ward off evil.

Excitedly they cross the lawn
And head straight toward the back,
Where there do stand a wooden bridge
Whose planks are worn and cracked.

The moon up high does light the way
Lest they should have some fear,
For many a times they came this way,
'Twas not their first time here.

But all and still there is an air
That does hold some foreboding,
As if a sign was held up high,
Thus saying, "Don't go for it."

Soon as they step onto the bridge,
An icy chill engulfs them.
Though quite out of the ordinary,
By no means do it stop them.

Now Tonie explains this with her logic.
"The temperature of the air
Indeed can be a whole lot cooler
When water is mixed in there."

Their given route across the water
Onto the other side
Do not take long and is familiar.
There is no need for fright.

The Haunted Forest

But once they reached the other side,
Everything they know does change.
They look around and see that things
Are not as they so planned.

Their path behind do not give way
For them to turn around,
So they are forced to travel on
And venture unknown ground.

Between one another, they give forth comfort
To help themselves along;
But all of them are very scared,
Heard clearly in their tones.

But if they are to make it through,
They know they must be strong,
And so they march with dignity,
Embraced all arm in arm.

The nightly sounds, all forest new,
Are strange to them by far.
The moon is full, but it would help
If they could get some stars.

Now in this place, imagination,
It takes them for a ride.
With all the sights and sounds about,
Their minds want to go wild.

Ann breaks the silence, the first to speak.
"Hey, did you guys hear that?
It sounds to me like galloping hoofs,
Going softly pitty-pat."

"Now, listen, Ann, it's hard enough
We're out here in the woods.
The comment that you're making now,
It will do us no good.

Let's keep our focus on the path,
Pushing ourselves ahead.
The sounds we hear are bad enough
Without you adding dread."

So with restraint Ann holds her peace
And follows them as well,
Both hoping that she did not hear
The sound of tolling bells.

They make their way a little further,
Then Tonie calls a halt.
The turn is hers to now speak out
And stop them in the dark.
"Hark, give an ear and listen now
And tell me what you hear."

And Tommie says, "It's very clear
There's nothing here to hear."
Then with a frown as pale as paste,
She nods her confirmation.
"That's just the point. There is no sound,
Nothing incarnation."

It strikes them, then like sickled ice,
Their hearts now beating as one.
A strangled cord deep in their throats
Is blaring out a warning.

They all turn around in one smooth motion,
Peering into the darkness,
Staring by far to glimpse some source
That life has not departed.

A darkness thick as black burned gravy
Does size the atmosphere,
And far beyond a hopeless night,
Their bodies are webbed with fear.

With straining eyes and fragile limbs,
They are entranced in blackness.
And haunting voices in their heads
Squeeze with chilling tightness.

THE HORSEMAN FIRST ENCOUNTER

Then suddenly their mood does change.
The spell is finally broken;
For in the distance they hear a sound,
No doubt a very good token.

They brace themselves as the sound increase,
Preparing for their rescue.
From tiny puttering tap, tap, tap,
It all plays out on cue.

For in the distance their eyes do spot
A tiny flickering glow,
And as they thus continue traveling,
The flicker also grows.

Then in a flash out of nowhere,
A figure spew in sight.
And what they see no lens can snap,
Nor can no word describe.

Seated high in all his glory,
Mounted upon a stallion,
Reared back high and holding its head
Like a golden prize medallion,

None other than the headless horseman,
Dressed totally down in black
From head to toe, not only that
But a flowing cape attached.

It bellows out like a serpentine,
Poised and ready to strike,
That has his victims all lined up
Struck motionlessly with fright.

Hot fiery breath steams from the nose
Of his teeth-baring stallion
That towers above them with prancing hoofs,
Which stretches toward the heaven.

But worst of all what meets their eyes
Is the pumpkin in his hand,
Its flaming head and ghastly grin
Wider than the usual span.

And in this moment, they know for sure
Their lives are about to end
As they do huddle tight arm in arm,
The loyalist of three friends.

They say their prayers, their eyes alight
In the silence roundabout.
As the headless horseman takes his time
To snuff their lives clear out.
But in the space of this dilemma,
There is a pertinent change.
In this last hour of their demise,
Inside they become deranged.

Between the span that started when
The pumpkin is lifted in hand
Unto the demise of three friends' heads,
Sanity leaves the plane.

As the pumpkin head is zooming in
About to make the kill,
There comes a rumbling growling sound
By a driven will to live.

The nearby sounds are theirs in one,
Of Tonie, Ann, and Tommie,
Whose stomachs growl in desperation
For something good and yummy.

The fear that once sized up their souls
Has now been changed all right
To taste and eat their main dessert
A good old pumpkin pie.

A savage glint now fill their eyes,
No longer are they afraid;
But now it is the headless horseman,
Who now will join the dead.
Right then and there he senses the change
While they set forth a table
Upon a tree stump there besides them
With silverware and spreadings.

Indeed, they are no more the victims
In this forsaken world.
Time to get straight down to business,
It's no more, boys and girls.

And when the horseman sees this change,
He's seized with fear so cold.
His plans before indeed now change,
For it is time to go.

Those glowing forks and shining knives,
He sees them gripping tight
Do spark in him a desperation
That summoned all his might.

At this moment, the valiant stallion
Turn tail and flee away,
Leaving the flaming pumpkin head
To live another day.

But seeing the craving, starved set faces
Igniting the trio's eyes,
Now the only thing set on their minds:
"Wow! Dinner has arrived."
And scared now stiff in one smooth motion
Without the slightest pause,
The pumpkin head just twists around
And leaves them each and all.

And in that moment of awkward retreat,
A horror strikes the friends.
To let the pumpkin head escape
Would sign their bitter end.

THE CHASE

So with all haste, the chase is on
And what a sight to see.
The headless horseman chased by his head,
Chased by a teen of three.

With thundering hoofs and flaming mane,
The horseman gallops away,
Covering ground as fast as he can
To reach his home in haste.

In hot pursuit, gaining as well,
The pumpkin head makes gain,
Fast pulling itself toward its mark,
Thus pulling up the train.

And last of all and scurrying behind,
Our trio muster all,
Clearing the trees, the rocks, the brushes,
Along with all pitfalls.

The chase goes on, a strive for life
Of which must soon be won,
Here in this do-or-die situation,
Which is by no means fun.

But finally, the climax comes.
This quarry is about to shift;
And this is where they all do stand,
Approaching the wooden bridge.

Indeed, this is as sayings go,
Where rubber meets the road,
Or all the stuff do hit the fan.
Let loose and let it go.

The headless horseman only needs
To make it to the bridge,
And he will be scot-home-free,
Away from these crazed kids.

The pumpkin head must also make
A bodily connection
Upon the bridge to free itself
From these wild teens' obsession.

Tonie and Ann and Tommie too
Also have much at stake.
They have to get that pumpkin head
Or die here in this place.

Now everyone is moving fast.
There is no time to think.
Their timing at this bridge must be
Most perfectly in sync.
The hour is here; the time is now.
What more is there to say?
It happens fast and all at once,
As if being wrenched awake.

The headless horseman hits the bridge.
His flaming head comes next,
And in the rear our trio moves
As fast to break their necks.

Alas, it's seen in Tonie's eyes,
As well as Tommie too.
They won't be able to make the grade.
They know this time they're through.

To make it worse, coming from the rear,
Ann shoots out of nowhere.
She knocks them down sliding on the ground,
Then takes off through the air.

Knocked on their buns, they simply stare
And watch Ann do her thing,
Sailing high up toward the river's edge
With waving arms and screams.

It is too bad it ends this way,
No time for them to say
Their love goodbye with smiling faces,
Which always kept them straight.
Oh wow, oh wow, they did not make it,
A tragic end by far,
Yet everything did light up bright
Before it all went dark.

The Meal

Upon the ground, there lies three bodies
As stiff as stiff can be.
Tonie's stretched out with Ann's beside.
Tommie in the middle makes three.

These unmarked graves above the soil,
Oh, will they ever be found?
But suddenly, the silence breaks
With a startling laughing sound.

"Oh wow, ah man, what can I say?
That pie was so delicious.
You did not tell us you could cook.
Of this we weren't suspicious."

"Oh, it was nothing," Tommie says,
As a blush rise in his face.
'Twas something I did given our need,
Just put together in haste.

With bellies filled and decent rest,
They're on their way once more,
But this time with much happier moods
As Tonie moves them forward.

Their silent track is not too bad,
Although few words are said.
And thus they make very good progress,
Considering they are well-fed.

Tonie cannot help as they track on
To give forth a small giggle,
Which they all hear and wonder about
Saying, "What is she now figuring?"

"Oh, I was thinking about the odds
Of what you did back there,
The way you dived and caught that head
Simultaneously in the air."

Then Tommie adds, "Yeah, that was wow,
The way you slid on by,
Coming in low and springing up hard,
Then shooting up toward the sky.

If not for you, we would have lost
Everything in that wild chase.
But your quick thinking and taking action,
It put us in first place."

Then Tonie adds, "My tactics are good,
But, Ann, you did one better.
You planned it out and made the move,
And nothing else did matter."
Ann accepts the praise from her friends
Yet have to set them straight
And give account of the full story
Of how it all took place.

"Yea, as we ran fast as we could,
I couldn't keep up with y'all.
I saw as well all hope was gone,
And all had just been lost.

Ironically, it's hard to say.
But in that very last moment,
My foot got tangled in some vines,
And then I fell down tumbling.

And as I slid along the ground,
My hand became entangled.
I then was clutching a hanging vine,
That hung at an odd angle.

I found myself sailing through the sky,
Going up, up, and away,
Moving faster than I ever thought
With nothing to halt my stay.

Then suddenly the vine just snapped
And sent me flying wild.
And so I reached for anything,
Just hoping to stay alive.
Then in the black, out of the blue,
My eyes went fiery bright.
I felt a flare of singing heat,
Then everything blacked out."

"We will accept as you propose
That that's the way it happened,
But from our view which is quite clear,
That is not what we captured.

Indeed, this is what we did see
While running through the woods.
The chase was on, and we did run
With everything we could.

But as we ran and gave our all,
The horseman did by far
Began to pull away from us,
And all hope did seem lost.

With all our strength and power spent,
We knew this was the end,
So we resided to let it go.
But here's where you came in.

We heard you yell like Tarzan's wife,
Then from the rear you came.
You grabbed a vine from off the ground.
From there you went insane.
You knocked us flat onto the ground,
And then took charge of all.
Into the sky you left us sitting,
Flat on our bum-bum sprawled.

You traversed the air with grace and speed
And aimed your target true.
And toward the headless horseman ride,
Your body toward him you threw.

And as you flipped head over heels,
You gave a warrior's cry.
Then reached out for the pumpkins head,
Quite heedless of its fire.

Your timing on point, your angle right,
The pumpkin head you grabbed,
Then veered away into the brush
And let the stallion pass.

When once across the bridge at bay,
The horseman couldn't return,
He took the loss, counted the cost,
And swore revenge in turn.

But after this feat, you in turn
Was exhausted to the hilt.
You were out cold with food in tow,
So we gave you a lift.
You renewed our hearts and revived our spirit.
So we went back to camp,
Where Tommie did the rest from there
With a meal straight off the ramp."

THE BRIDGE

As long as we do stick together
No matter what comes our way,
We know that we will make it through
To see another day.

They all agree and keep on moving
On through the forest night,
Believing in heart and knowing for sure
It soon will be all right.

And true at last their patience pays,
They come unto a clearing.
Purged of debris of the haunted forest,
Their eyes are almost tearing.

Two oak trees stand at the clearing's edge,
Sentinel to a bridge
That stretches ahead both far and long
Unto another ridge.

And there across the other side,
A castle they do see.
To them it is a joyous sight,
And oh, what a relief.

Oh, now there is a rescue flag,
A beacon in the night,
A path that they can safely take
And make all things all right.

But once they reached the entrance way
Of the bridge that they will cross,
Their hearts do plummet down to their stomachs,
And all their jawbones drop.

The wooden bridge is rotten and worn,
And many planks are gone.
And when the wind does pass through them,
It hums a death hymn song.

Beneath this outstretched bridge of horror
Awaited an endless abyss
To suck them down and keep their souls
If any of them dare slip.

They stop abruptly in their tracks.
A decision must be made:
To chicken out and stay right here
Or cross and prove they're brave.

It's one on two, a decision made
They all do not agree.
Both Ann and Tonie decide to across,
Leaving Tommie at the tree.
As big and brave a man he is,
They cannot change his mind.
There is no reason nor strong debate,
No coaxing they can find.

Their hearts do break to leave him here,
So this is what they plan.
They will cross over and find a way
To bring him to that land.

With hugs and kisses short and sweet,
They say farewell for now.
They let him know they will be back.
Do count this as a vow.

Their first step on the bridge is bad.
A plank decides to fall.
They halt their track to hear the echo,
Which never is recalled.

But bracing themselves, they move on forward,
Each step being carefully placed.
Though they're concerned, they dare not turn
To look at Tommie's face.

But second by second and moment by moment,
They keep a steady pace
Against the wind that knock them hard
To seal a tragic fate.
Oh, Tonie does feel, with trembling limbs,
Ann's terrible pain for Tommie
But reminds her that he did decide.
Indeed, he was not coming.

But Tonie concedes in the end,
And this she let Ann know:
"When we are safe, I will go back
Even If I must use rope."

This fills Ann with much assurance,
For Tonie she can trust.
So with this settled, they move on forward,
Plowing through moss and dust.

Tommie is ashamed; what can he do?
He loves his two dear friends,
But there's a fear he can't control
That wins out in the end.

Here in the dark, he sits in fear
And look out over the bridge,
And longing to be there at their sides
Is now his deep-down wish.

He wrestles with his inner fears
Alone and in the dark.
Immobilized, he cannot move.
He has no fire or spark.
He's in the dark; silence surrounds him,
Which now is very ominous.
For every living thing has hushed,
As though the second coming.

No birds, no bees, no wind, no breeze.
As Tommie listens hard,
He cannot help it; there is something
Lurking in the dark.

Afraid to look, not able to help,
From the bridge he turns away
And looks again to their traveled path
Of which he is now prey.

It is at first so very faint,
A sound that's barely heard,
But then grows louder and recognizable,
Which chills his every nerve.

There's in the distance a galloping sound,
A small growing spark as well,
Heading straight toward him in determination,
As if straight out of hell.

The fear before, which held him fast,
Has now gone out the window
At the headless horseman's spoken words,
Which he now does remember.
A sworn oath given, he had declared.
He would pay all them back,
For what they did unto him then,
Indeed, this was a fact.

Like a lightning bolt that's on the move,
Tommie gives no place for dying.
Once at the tree trunk balled up tight
No more, but now he's flying.

He hit the bridge at top full speed,
No heed to its condition,
But runs in fear of his own life.
He now is on a mission.

And though the planks beneath his feet
Give way due to his weight.
This does not stop or slow his plight
As the bridge violently shakes.

He has one thing upon his mind.
He wants to stay alive
Despite the snaps of twining rope
Of which the bridge is tied.

Now near the end close to the edge,
The girls do see some hope
Until they hear the rattling sounds,
The snapping of the ropes.
'Tis all at once they feel the vibes
Their feet beneath them give
And, in that instant, turn around
And give face to their fears.

THE MONSTER ATTACK

Now from the dark and coming fast,
A monster they do see,
With lightning speed and muscled built,
Then the bridge gives under feet.

Now finally the moment's come,
And death they will now meet
By plunging down so far below
Into that endless deep.

It is not easy as they are slammed
And gripped first by the beast.
It grabs them both and takes them high
To assail them from the deep.

Their breath now gone, gripped by the claws
That squeeze their helpless limbs.
As it tumbles them onto the ground,
They can but just give in.

Slammed down hard, they await the pain
The claws will now inflict.
Instead, they are completely shocked,
Seeing who the monster is.

With wheezing breath and laughter wild,
"Hello, dear Ann and Tonie,
Would I be wrong to offer you
A lift in this very moment?"

A glee, a frown, a smile, a pout,
And much more shone at once
As well in tone as their faces belie
When both their voices launch.

We thought you dead, torn into pieces,
Attacked by some wild beast,
Then thought that we were next in line
To make for a great feast.

Upon the ground, they lay sometime,
Just gathering up their wits.
So glad to be alive together
With joy that now exists.

Now Tonie first as usual is
Regroup from this ordeal
But have to drag Tommie from Ann's grip
To chill what she does feel.

They made it through another saga.
They're on their feet again
As they approach the castle's doors
Against the howling wind.

Castle Safe

On either side as they approach
The stairs unto the door,
Bouquets of flowers as red as blood
Bloom with outstretched roses.

Not only strong unto the eyes
But also to the smell,
The aroma is of copper iron,
As though fire burned in hell.

But once they reached the very top
Before the double doors,
So delicate it is engraved.
They dared to touch its oars.

But with ominous clouds and needing help,
This outside atmosphere
Does spur them on to now gain entrance
To what awaits them here.

As Tonie and Tommie turn briefly away,
Ann oh so lightly knocks.
Then suddenly the doors explode,
And off their hinges pop.

They both fly inward with lots of noise,
And bang, they hit the floor
And stir up dust so thick and strong.
Clean air is now no more.

They spit and choke and try to breathe
As filth do fill their lungs.
They did not know their entrance here
Would cause so much alarm.

When they are able to breathe once more,
They attack Ann both together.
"We did not mean for you to pound
And cause the doors to shatter."

But Ann protests, "It wasn't me.
I did not throw a fit.
There has to be another force
To stir up all of this."

They take a breath; they're all too tense.
They have to work this out.
So arm in arm, they enter in,
Prepared to look about.

To say, "Oh wow, Oh man, Oh man,"
By no means do come close.
The gorgeousness of this great hall
Is beyond one's greatest hope.
Antique paintings and lifelike statues
And priceless artifacts
Align the octagon-shaped room,
Arrayed with other crafts.

They stand stock still in the vestibule,
Their mouths agape wide open,
Trying to access this given space,
Wide-eyed with minds unfocused.

There to their left a stairwell starts
And circle the entire room
And terminate high above their heads,
Where there a balcony looms.

Once over the shock, they case the place
To get a better feel
To see what place they now have entered
Deciding if it's good or ill.

Among the relics do Tonie find,
Galore of books to read.
Ann's glowing eyes spot twinkling items
To solve all money needs.

Tommie spies a centaur stature
That cradles a life-size girl.
Gagged and bound, she seems so real.
His stomach twist and twirl.

A GHOSTLY VISIT

While all of them are deeply lost,
Caught up in their own world,
A moaning sound is suddenly heard
Mixed in the air above.

When they look up, what should they see
Up twirling in the air?
But a semi-ghost taking form,
It's time to pay the fare.

The fear is great; they all divide.
Yea, each to his own way.
Ann is the first to run for shelter
And to the doors right straight.

She's disappointed when she gets there
To find them locked down tight
But doesn't stop or hesitate
To find a place to hide.

She chooses the place, the balcony
To make for her retreat.
The only flaw is how she does it.
She uses no stairs, you see.

She's at the door with no escape,
Then sees high ground above.
The very next moment, she's behind the seats
With all the curtains closed.

Now Tonie stands her ground quite firm,
Fascination in her eyes,
To get a better look at this.
What will materialize?

A Newfound Girlfriend

But Tommie is grasped by residual fright
And runs off in blind fear.
He doesn't look or even care
As long as it's not here.

He darts off wildly from the room
Through one of many doors.
He's moving fast with small concern
Of ceilings, walls, or floors.

Because of this, he hit a plank
That's rotten to its core.
His feet plunge through, his body in suit.
He's then sucked through the floor.

He yells, he screams, he tumbles, he falls.
A downward spiral he takes.
He's banged up good from a series of stairs
Before he hits the brakes.

And when he stops and finally halts,
It's with great consternation.
By hitting a door straight head on,
That seals his destination.

He feels a *smack* and hears a *crash*,
Then everything goes black.
With loss of time and scenery of place,
Everything is out of whack.

What is the span; what are the hours?
What time of day is it?
Or will the stars rise with the moon
And let the earth keep orbit?

Yes, Tommie awakes; he's still alive.
Life is quite good to him,
For what he sees in his sore vision
Is nothing less than heaven.

He's in the lap of a beautiful girl,
Who rocks him like a baby.
Her gentle coos and warming strokes
Have put him in a haven.

Into fathomless eyes big and round,
He stares up at her face.
With bloodred lips and jet-black hair,
He's in another place.

Her voice is honey, so sweet, so soft.
It nulls his pain away
As she rocks him gently with her hands
Pressed firmly to his face.
When his eyes do open with great concern,
Urgency fills her voice.
"Are you all right? I'm glad to see
You haven't been destroyed."

Her pleading eyes, they pierce his soul,
As well as her concern.
And this alone makes him feel better.
The table have now turned.

With groggy words and stuttering lips,
"Where am I? Who are you?
The last I know is I was running.
I then fell through a shoot."

Tommie's attitude does suddenly change
As he looks at himself.
His chest is bare; his shirt is gone.
Yea, have she no respect.

He now demands in a gruff tone,
"Indeed, who are you, girl,
And what have you done unto me
Here in this bizarre world?"

She's taken aback but hold her ground.
"How dare you speak to me.
It's I who should be asking you
Why are you here indeed."
A guilt of pain now passes through him
While looking into her eyes.
He should not have attacked her so.
He will apologize.

Excuse me, miss. I am quite sorry.
Being rude is not my game.
So please forgive me of my fault.
I am so quite ashamed.

The moment passed; there is no grudge
Between these two young people.
But now there is an alliance formed
Of which is now so needful.

I do accept your apologies,
And my name's Tabitha.
And my concern is for your health.
In this you can so relish.

He tries to move, but there is pain
That moves throughout his body,
So he falls back into her care
And thus flow with the folly.

She strokes his head which give relief,
And then she forges on.
"It's I who should be thanking you
For all that you have done."
A puzzled look besets his face
As he looks on in shock,
Trying to figure if she's sincere
Or if this is a mock.

She sees his shock, and then explains,
"You rescued me indeed.
I was before locked in this dungeon,
But now I am set free.

For when you barreled head fast straight on
And ran into the door,
You knocked it off of its strong hinges
And crashed it to the floor.

You stumbled in a few steps forward,
Then fell into a heap.
You were unconscious and in bad shape.
Your body burned with heat.

I removed your shirt to let it dry,
Then cared for you as such.
I prayed and hoped with all my might
That this would count for much.

I'm graceful that you have awoke.
You have my gratitude.
I'm in your debt, so ask of me
What is it I can do."

They now proceed on informal terms
To assess their situation.
And thus by them now working together,
They have a destination.

With intel knowledge of the castle's design,
She reunites the three
And bring together once again,
Tonie, Ann, and Tommie.

A Newfound Boyfriend

Before this happens while Tommie's away,
Both Ann and Tonie throw down.
And they, like Tommie, have walk the line.
They too a strange friend found.

When Ann did hide and Tommie did run,
Tonie just stood her ground
And watched the aberration form
From whence they heard the sound.

Lo and behold appeared a ghost
That hovered in the sky.
It then took form and glided down
To stand at Tonie's side.

She did not flinch; she did not cry
Nor lose her cool at all.
She thus instead engaged the former.
They then began to talk.

Many a things she did find out
Of which would be much help
To aid them in their hellish plight
And escape from this nightmare.

This ghostly figure whom she met
Was charming, to say the least.
With jet-black hair and charcoal eyes,
His build was very sleek.

He had a charm and dazzling smile,
Being cordial as could be.
Whether ghost or not, he'd surely make
The perfect boy indeed.

So while they chat and made themselves
As friendly as could be,
Ann hid up in the balcony,
Afraid what she might see.

But shortly, her curiosity,
It got the best of her,
And finally she dared to look
From behind the tight-drawn curtains.

And what she saw incited her.
She couldn't believe her eyes.
Tonie below was making good
With a gorgeous, beautiful guy.

What fear remained was then dismissed.
Ann got herself together.
Now using the stairs she did cut in
To be part of the chatter.
And thus they did converse as one,
A new trio being made,
Until in time when Tommie appeared
And at his side a maiden.

An Escape Plan

All chatter stopped upon their entrance.
A hush-hush filled the air
But leaping flames of jealousy
Do hotly fuel Ann's glare.

Now, no more seated on the couch,
Ann makes an interception,
Confronting Tommie and Tabitha,
Throwing away the welcome.

"And who is this, if I may ask?"
Ann shoots a bit abrupt.
"I see you took your precious time.
To find us, you didn't rush."

"Hold on, dear Ann. Don't jump the gun.
It's not what it seems like.
I got quite lost and hurt myself,
And she did help me out—"

"I bet she did," Ann interrupts,
"And that in many ways."
And with this, Tommie is suddenly,
Completely shocked and dazed.

Now Tonie sees the situation.
It's getting out hand.
She takes control and call a halt
With sharp, strong reprimand.

"Now, Ann dear girl, do get a grip,
And halt your imagination.
Let us be sound and give a space
Unto his explanation.

We have a plan to leave this place.
We must be unified.
We cannot let our petty feelings
Cause us to suicide.

So calm down now. Let's roll together,
And be adults in heart.
For we are friends to one another.
Let's not tear that apart.

With big deep breaths and lots of effort,
Ann gains her self-control
But still takes Tommie by the arm
And between him and Tab she stroll.

Now with the five all gathered around.
Revelations are revealed
As their brains pool to make a plan
To be rid of this evil.
Now Dwayne the ghost confides in Tonie
The origin of this castle.
It belongs unto none other than
Dracula, that old rascal.

Tommie swallows hard; his eyes stretch wide
To get free of their sockets.
Just how many monsters can this place
Pull out of its deep pockets?

The Library Lair

Weak in the knees with upset stomach,
Tommie's ready to throw the towel,
But then he gazes at Tabitha
And melts at her warm smile.

They learn also that Dwayne and Tab
Are brother and sister in blood,
Both bound unto this dreaded castle
Till someone pulls the plug.

Yea, all the fates are in the stars.
This is their lucky night.
With these strange visitors, a full moon,
Indeed, the time is right.

The plot does thicken as they go on.
They're given a curse to break.
A spell thus cast by Dracula himself,
Which keeps these children caged.

Dwayne is cursed as the castle's prisoner,
A ghost with chains and all,
To haunt its passages day and night,
Confined within its walls.

And Tab, poor girl, was locked below
Within the dungeon walls
To be thus beaten and also tortured
Despite her pleading calls.

Of course, this news is very bad.
It pains our trio so.
It's not their problem, but now it is
Because they want to go.

They have no choice says Tab and Dwayne.
This is their only choice.
"When we're curse-free, we'll have the means
To free you from this course."

Aside from this, Tommie feels a pain
That boils up deep inside.
To think of Tabitha being thus hurt,
He cannot let this slide.

The girls alike have their own reasons
For which to lend a hand.
They desperately like him as well
Want passage from this land.

So with all five now head-to-head,
They put the plan in play.
They have the means and all the tools
To make a get-a-way.
They have need of a special potion,
Which Tabitha can make,
But first they must get to the library
Before this can take place.

Smart as a whip, Tab knows this place,
As if it's her own hand,
As well also the formula
With words at her command.

And through a maze of corridors,
They finally reach the room.
It's creepy and old and worn and new.
It's full of webs and gloom.

There's rows and rows of books galore
With shelves from top to bottom.
It catches Tonie in its lure.
This place is now quite solemn.

Yea, in the center of the floor,
There stands a podium tall,
A tree grown plant straight from the ground
Supported by roots and all.

A cauldron sits off to one side
So black it hurts the eyes.
Its three prong legs support its weight
Suspended over fire.
Set in the wall, a five-pane window,
Which leads to the outside,
Which have one of its multipane
Missing in the night.

Indeed, there are many other items
That decorate this room.
They range from weird to out of sight,
Touched with a cloak of doom.

No time to waste, Tab grabs a book
With Tonie at her heel.
Instructing Tommie, he grabs a jug,
And the cauldron he does fill.

Tonie and Tabitha are like mad scientists,
Gathering ingredients needed
To make the potion they will need
To set our trio free.

And as the concoction slowly brew,
Their tension seems to ease.
Then Dwayne take time to run an errand
And floats up with the breeze.

He slowly unsolidify
Right there before their eyes,
Slides smoothly toward the broken window,
And then is gone outside.
This very change, it sends a chill,
Along all of their spines,
Though they've seen it once before.
It's likely again in time.

As Tabitha reads and Tonie stirs,
A fog rise from the pot.
As Ann and Tommie on the other side
Stand rooted in their spots.

Of how much time do pass on by,
On this they have no thought,
But they are brought back to their senses
By a very horrific shock.

A piercing scream, it streaks the air,
As if all hell broke loose.
Then suddenly the streak does halt,
As if choked with a noose.

Hot goosebumps and all their cousins
Grip Tonie, Ann, and Tommie.
Their stomachs churn, and insides twist,
Not knowing what is coming.

But Tabitha merely cocks her head,
Not rattled even one bit.
"Oh, that is just some screeching owl,
And we are used to it.
So don't you worry your pretty little heads.
All's going according to plan.
With just a few more things to do,
Your moment will be at hand."

Their nerves once more now on the level
And Dwayne having now returned,
A noted change is on his face,
That's now robust and firm.

Tonie now notice him all the more
As if a fat hooked worm.
As he steps into Tabitha's place,
Who winks at him in turn.

I do believe the rest of you
Can take care of this task
As I attend to other matters
That we might finish at last.

Then Tab continues and turns to Tommie.
"I'll need your helping hands
To lift and move some heavy things
In completing all our plans."

She doesn't wait but grasps his hand,
And then they're out the door,
Thus leaving Dwayne and Tonie there,
With Ann's mouth to the floor.
Ann holds her breath and quenches her anger.
She won't let this get to her.
It's just a temporary thing.
They'll be back in a hurry.

THE LOVE CONNECTION

All business like with minor chatter,
Tabitha leads the way.
They pass through winding corridors,
Which makes the perfect maze.

They find themselves in an upward path
To reach their destination.
A storage room is where they're headed,
Arriving at their location.

She opens the door and gestures him in.
He looks about the room.
Indeed, there are so many utensils,
And even a witch's broom.

He would browse if time permitted,
But he is on a mission.
"So what's in here, Miss Tabitha?
What is it we are missing?

You say you need my help in tow.
Now tell me what's the plan."
She smiles at him and grasps his hand.
"I need you for these cans."

Her smile is warm; her tone is soft
As she points toward the wall,
Where there are lined up cans of paint,
Two short rows three feet tall.

"This is the blood paint we will need
To make our pentagram.
We'll almost there; we'll near the end.
Indeed, this will be grand.

He braces himself and takes a hold
To holster a few cans.
To his surprise, he finds them heavy.
That gives him cause to strain.

He understands why she needs help
To finish up their quest.
And he is more than happy to
Do all that she does ask.

She walks ahead with him in tow,
Their task now nearly completely.
But Tommie finds it quite disturbing,
Seeing her bum-bum swishing.

He's both relieved, and then surprised
When Tab comes to a halt.
She shyly smiles and enters a door
After she lightly knocks.
With a puzzled face and a knot-tied tongue,
With a question, Tommie croaks,
"And why are we now stopping here?
We should keep on the go."

"We have the paint, but we do need
The brushes just as well.
So why don't you put those cans down
And rest them near the stairs?"

"Do come with me into the room
To get our very last item.
We will be quick and on our way.
There is no need to idle."

With great relief, he bids her wish
And sets the paint cans down.
But when he steps into the room,
Now should he smile or frown?

This is not a utility room
As he had first supposed.
But instead, it is a Harlem lair,
Adorned with lilies and roses.

His mind a gasp, he cannot speak,
Standing rooted in the door.
Knowing indeed she have deceived him,
An anger within him rose.
A big love bed sit in the center,
Adorned with ornate charms,
A draping canopy with silky curtains,
And pillows soft and warm.

Its apple shape entices the eyes,
Just like the Garden of Eden.
The entire décor of the room
Is set for smooth deceiving.

When finally, he finds his voice,
It vibes with angry tones.
"I thought you said we came in here
For brushes then we're done?"

"Indeed, they're here within the closet
Behind that other door.
Oh, do go on and get them now,
And then we'll leave this floor."

Her voice is smooth with no inflections.
His tone does not disturb her.
Instead, she's filled with anticipation
And with a little mirth in it.

Tommie holds his peace, moving to the closet,
And there began his search,
His temper rising at the thought,
Of now being used by her.
But in default, he has to stop
When he sees the brushes
Tucked far away back in the corner.
They're new, unused, untouched.

He knows that he must once again
Apologize to her.
He doesn't know why it's hard for him
To give her his best worth.

He pulls together what he must do
To say how sorry he is
Until he turns and looks about
To see what is revealed.

There in the buff with no clothes on
Stands Tabitha upright.
With twinkling eyes and a dazzling smile,
With teeth that are gleaming white.

He suddenly stops; his mouth goes dry.
He finds it hard to breathe.
He's captivated by her eyes
As she moves forth with ease.

As she moves forward, he moves back,
Keeping a good safe distance.
Her voice is soft and like a purr
As if now ready for kissing.
"Now, come on, Tommie, let's have some fun.
Now that we're all alone.
Just you and I working together,
A lot we can get done."

"I like you, Tab. You're very cute.
You're beautiful in fact.
But if I do what you want me to,
That just would not be right."

She's not put off but keeps approaching
As he himself retreat.
"Oh, come on, Tommie, let's have some fun,
And play with all of me."

With every step, he does resist.
But gazing into her eyes,
It's like he's moving in slow motion,
Carried by watery tides.

Forward she slides with curved perched lips
To make that final move.
To his dismay he hits a wall.
There's nothing he can do.

All of a sudden, he's tumbling back,
Free falling toward the floor.
But he forgoes a terrible crash,
Sprawled in the bed of roses.
Flat on his back, laid on the bed,
He's at a loss at first.
But by the time he does recover,
Upon him is Tabitha perched.

Her grip is strong; her touch is soft
As Tommie struggles wild.
But all his efforts are brought to naught
As he gazes into her eyes.

He finds himself in a sea of passion,
Though this is not his wish.
He finds himself completely covered
By very warm lips and kisses.

The Love Bite

The girls alone with Dwayne, the ghost,
Are finishing up the task
Of brewing the potion to its peak
Before going into a flask.

A fuzzy haze floats from the pot,
Erupting between the two,
Ann's on one side, Tonie the other,
Standing there with Dwayne too.

Caught in a trance, Ann stares at Tonie.
And what she sees is off.
For Tonie's neck is in Dwayne mouth
With pointed fangs atop.

Ann gasps in shock as Tonie yelps.
And then she blinks her eyes.
She hears a slap of hand on flesh,
Then opens her eyes wide.

Ann is surprised; there's nothing there.
There's only Tonie and Dwayne.
Tonie rubs her neck as if in pain.
"Mosquitos," Dwayne explain.

Ann know her nerves are about to go,
Seeing things that are not there.
She needs to get out of this place.
She needs to get some air.

And with a poof, they now obtain
The crystal powder needed,
Whereby they might capture Dracula
And from this place be freed.

Now here is where the plan gets shaky.
And Tonie must use her wits.
For one of them must take the dare
And walk the castle naked.

The Twisted Bait

Their plan is this: they must lure Dracula
Here back into the library.
And with that done, they'll use the powder,
Then all is peachy and cherry.

But which of them will be the one
To walk the castle stripped
To dangle themselves like a piece of meat,
Being beautiful and being hip?

There is debate between the two.
Tonie and Ann have words.
But clever Tonie tilts the balance,
By tossing in a curve.

"It would be easy if Tommie was here,
For then he could so choose.
But he is off with Tabitha,
Doing what it is they do.

There is no doubt, Ann. You look great,
But Tab's a looker too.
If Tommie by chance just happens to see you,
Don't mean he'll change his view."

A jealous glint winks in Ann's eyes.
"I'll show you that's not true."
Ann makes her move and starts to strip,
Revealing skin so smooth.

When she is finished, she is adorned
In sexy lingerie.
With two thumbs-up, she smiles at Tonie.
Their plan is underway.

It is at first that Ann's long strides
Are confident and sure.
But all of this change bit by bit,
Walking through the corridors.

With high emotions at the moment,
She'd felt invincible,
But as she walks, adrenaline lost,
None of this seems sensible.

There was a route with given instructions
Of which path she should take.
Just hold it together and keep it cool,
And all would fall in place.

Now creaking floors and eerie sounds
Do haunt her every step.
And though her blood is racing hot,
She dares not call for help.
She must be brave and see it through,
For Tommie's sake at least.
When he finds out what she has done,
Within his arm she'll be.

With nerves of steel, she forces herself
To stay upon the path.
A little bit further, and then she'll have
Completed the route at last.

Now finally her heart slows down.
She's at the junction point.
A few more steps she'll turn around,
Sure as a pig goes "oink."

But suddenly she feels a prick
That's ebbing at her neck.
She doesn't think nor hesitate
But floors it to the deck.

She is so fast that Dracula
Is taken by surprise,
Being disappointed he only gets
A snap of air to bite.

And now that Ann has turned about.
It's Dracula she sees
As she hears the boom of clamping jaws
Made by his snapping teeth.
She steps away, her body trembling
With cold, cold chills of sweat.
Her eyes are wide, their sockets big,
Pure fear she has just met.

She tries to scream as she staggers back
From Dracula's approaching clutch.
She finds at hand there is a problem.
Her vocal cords are stuck.

As both of them stand motionless,
Dracula enjoys the view.
He siphons in her gorgeous body,
So tasteful; his mouth drools.

Now petrified unable to move,
He spears Ann with his eyes.
Now what did Dwayne and Tabitha say,
Don't look into his eyes.

She's almost smitten; what saves the day
Is the mirror behind her foe.
The reflection shows Ann's image alone,
This is what keeps her focus.

Arms at his sides, he moves in closer.
Still, Ann's unable to move.
He closes the distance within arm's reach,
Savoring this delicious food.
A full-face grin with long wolf's fangs,
Teeth not yet stained with blood,
He makes his move and reaches for Ann
To give her a bear hug.

A tasty treat this is indeed,
The finest of all wines.
Copper-fresh and soothingly sweet,
No better way to dine.

A deep fixation, a passion complete,
A vampire's day's delight,
It is the ultimate satisfaction,
One's darkest dream alight.

And such indeed would be the case
If not for one little thing,
Ann does not give herself away
To Dracula's deep whelm.

He never gets the chance to taste
The delicacies of Ann.
When he reaches for her, she is gone
Like the air blown in the rain.

At the very last moment as quick as lightning,
She slips right through his hands,
Leaving only a whiff of her sweet fragrance,
Moving blindly as she ran.
Coming to her senses spurred on by fear,
She aimlessly does run
Through the castle maze of corridors
With all her nerves undone.

Being chased by Dracula and running fast,
Ann dashes for her life.
With silent steps and a very loud voice,
She hopes help will arrive.

Her nakedness means nothing now
As she slips through the darkness,
As Dracula's steps echoes behind her,
Making her a target.

Needless to say, she's scared to death.
It's not what she had planned.
She'd trapped herself through jealousy,
Worrying about a man.

Now's not the time to cry and fret.
Ann pulls it all together.
It's now that she does note the silence,
As well as her pursuer's steps.

The silence is worse; indeed, it is
Than being chased as she was.
Deep in her heart, she silently prays,
Now seeking help from above.
She's hot and heated and flustered as well,
Decreasing her earlier pace.
She turns around and looks about
To front him face-to-face.

But in the darkness, she sees nothing,
Through squinting eyes alight.
He is not there; he can't be heard,
Which only increases her fright.

Now walking backward so cautiously,
Searching frantically,
She continues to scout everywhere she can,
Looking for clarity.

At last she backs herself into,
A castle's entrance way.
And at this point, she loses it all,
When she does see his face.

Her blood now boils; her head aches sore.
She's then grabbed from behind.
These icy fingers break all her will.
She's just run out of time.

The full moon face of Dracula
Looms big before her eyes.
His pale white skin, knife-stabbing eyes
Lean more than a surprise.
Captured by his sunken sockets,

She's completely paralyzed.
Also entranced by his ruby lips
That ride on cheekbones high.

But seeing those thirsty razor fangs
Inviting her warm neck,
She never imagined an end like this,
A mythical creature text.

Her vision is darkened as Dracula approaches
To take that final bite.
Ann offers her neck with her final sight
Of a bright rainbow of bursting light
Being followed by eternal blackness.

And with her final breath of will,
Of Tommie and Tonie she thinks.
Whatever happens she knows for sure,
Forever they will be linked.

Temptation Thwarted

He is enjoying those full round lips
That prick his strong firm neck
Until there's heard a shrieking cry
Within the castle's sect.

This shilling cry brings Tommie back
Unto his natural senses,
Thus dissolving his playtime with Tabby,
Which causes him to wince.

Back in the world he finds himself
Pressed body to body with Tab.
Worse even still, he's shirtless at that
And pressed against her breasts.

He knows in heart this will not do.
It's wrong on every count,
And even more he knows that scream.
It is his friend, Ann's, sound.

Indeed, before the regrettable
Can occur between the two,
Tommie suddenly springs off Tab
And does what he must do.

Now leaving Tab upon the bed,
Sprawled in her naked glory,
He dresses himself, not looking back,
And heads straight for the door.

But if he had but turned about
To glimpse her facial mask.
Her disappointment would have cut him
As deep as any glass.

But just as well he did not see
Her animalistic glare
Of which vindictively did swear,
His every limb she'd tear.

But Tommie's thoughts were for Ann only.
As he raced through the castle,
He instinctively finds the very same library
From whence he had thus left them.

And on his route, concerned for Ann,
He went through the main room
And lost his footing and thought for sure
That he was totally doomed.

He sailed up high into the air
And came down out of breath.
His life was saved uncanningly
By the full-life centaur statue.
He fell into its empty arms,
As safe as a little baby.
Though only a moment, something was off,
Something dark and shady.

But there's no time to reason it out.
Ann is his main concern.
As quick as lightning, he's up and off,
And rubber does he burn.

But all at once, once at the door,
He comes to a full halt
When he sees Ann lying on the floor,
Motionless on the spot.

Tonie is poised in solemn prayer,
Bent hovering over Ann's body.
Poor Ann is gone, and Tommie's heart breaks.
He feels it's all his fault.

THE BIG CATCH CAUGHT

Tommie slowly steps into the room
On wobbly legs no less,
And then he kneels and turns toward Ann,
On whom his teary eyes rest.

He says to Tonie, "Oh, what went wrong?"
She turns mechanically slow.
She is monotone, "Why, nothing at all,"
In an atmosphere too cold.

Tommie is confused and follows her gaze,
Now looking over his shoulder,
Where she's transfixed to the corner of the room,
Where something has hold of her.

He follows her gaze, unable to move.
His limbs stiffen like iron rods
Upon seeing the figure sitting in a chair,
As if he is a god.

It's Dracula, content, composed,
A haunted grin in place,
With paralyzing eyes and will-control
Showing upon his face.

Tommie is knelt, glued in his tracks,
A helpless victim at best,
Just only a puppet to be ripped to bits,
Like pieces of mangled flesh.

Or even worse, he may become,
A thoughtless, apathetic zombie
Who's mind-controlled by Dracula's power,
Like his dear friend here, Tonie.

The only thing that he can do
Is wait for the attack.
So patiently he stills himself
And stays where he is at.

Tommie's baffled that he doesn't attack
And get this over with.
"Instead of coming at me now
And make it fast and quick."

Dazed and confused, he looks from Dracula
And into Tonie's eyes.
She says, "You now look scared to death.
Indeed, what a surprise.

But if you can stop staring at him
And help me out with Ann,
I would indeed appreciate
If you'd lend a helping hand."
To this she adds a curt "Thank you"
That causes his jaw to drop.
It's then she sees the perplexity
That he is very lost.

Their time is short; she makes it quick,
Giving to him some details.
"Ann lured Dracula to the library.
All things did go quite well.

We used the potion they had us make,
As Tabitha and Dwayne said.
Ann backed herself into the room,
And Dracula she led.

He suddenly came from nowhere
And caught us by surprise.
Fortunately, in time I grabbed her
And pulled her to the side.

I threw the powder in his face
Right just before Ann screamed,
Then Dracula dropped onto the floor,
As if in a dazed dream.

I moved him there into that chair,
Then came to check on Ann.
Then you came zooming in right after,
Fast as a flying plane."
There is a gloat of fascination
That's written all over her face
As she relates these strange events
Of what have taken place.

Tommie looks at Tonie for a moment,
Then muses to himself,
Whew, this is just the way she is.
She can be no one else.

THE COMFORT SPELL

Now satisfied with the explanation
Of what has taken place,
He still looks down in wonderment
At dear Ann's pitiful face.

And there she lies seductively,
Poised upon the floor.
As he and Tonie move to assist her,
She now began to stir.

Tommie looks at Ann then back at Tonie,
Now struck by the realization
As he asks of her in a secretive tone,
"Why's Ann lying here naked?"

His voice does waver as he tries to keep
Modesty and control
As Tommie make his inquiries of
The whereabouts of Ann's clothes.

But Tonie whispers, "A later date,
We'll discuss it all in time."
She takes this as an affirmative
And turns back on a dime.

It's at this point Ann fully recovers
And slowly open her eyes.
The very first person she happens to see
Is Tommie to no surprise.

She flings her arms about him tightly
For comfort and security
In a trembling voice. "Tommie, it was horrible,"
As she then starts to weep.

He comforts her with a soothing voice.
"Oh, Tommie, hold me tight."
Then he wraps his arms about her body.
"Dear Ann, it'll be all right."

With passing time, he gently strokes
Her body soft and warm,
With gentle fingers combing her hair
To ease her rising alarm.

And Ann in turn reciprocates
With one hand on his chest.
The other in graceful circular motion
Along his spine does rest.

A sparkle now is in Ann's eyes.
Indeed, she is okay,
And so is Tommie in this love nest,
It's time to put things straight
So Tonie retorts in a very sharp tone,
"It's time for us to go!"
Ann hesitates to get her clothes
Until Tonie uses more force.

"Get up right now. We have to go.
Get clothed, and let's move out!"
With one quick hug, she let him go,
Then she's moving about.

RESOLVED ISSUES

Things back to normal, Tommie asks,
"Oh, where might Dwayne now be?"
"There's a few last things he had to do
Whereby we can be freed."

And with this statement now confirmed,
This next thing Tonie does offer,
"And that was just before Miss Beauty
Did scream her little head off."

Then Tommie says with anticipation,
"Wow, I can hardly wait,
Just knowing indeed that very soon,
We'll be free of this place."

"And do you think we'll really get free?"
Asks Ann being pessimistic.
Respectively speaking Tonie and Tommie,
"Dwayne and Tabitha said it."

Then Tonie goes on, "I venture to say
All will work for the best."
And Tommie nods, "So good so far."
Ann, "I'm not sure of that."

"Now stop the skepticism, Ann.
We're wasting precious time."
Ann incites, "Speaking of time,
Did Tabby and you do fine?"

A trace of jealousy is in Ann's voice,
Which is no big surprise.
Given the ordeals they've encountered,
It seems they're back on track.

He hoped as much the girls had not
Brought up the deal with Tab.
A very compromising subject
Is now put on his tab.

His mind races back in different ways
Of what had really happened.
How can he tell them the ordeal
Of him and Tabitha?

Was it his fault? He blushes hotly.
He tries for a straight face.
Going eye to eye, what shall he say,
His thoughts in a wild race?

Now with his stomach turning in knots,
He finally resigns
To tell it all and let it go,
Saying, "Well, to be quite honest—"
"Yes, we finished what we had to."
Tabitha's voice chimes in,
Finishing his sentence oh so smoothly
Like a choir in the wind.

Composed and relieved, Tommie looks around
As Tabby approaches his side.
Discrete, unnoticed by the girls,
Tabitha pats his backside.

This suggestive tag has implications,
Which Tommie knows all too well.
Now unto her he owes a debt
For which he does not care.

Now all of them have put aside
All conflicts from before.
Their only goal and final task
Is home sweet home, you know.

They carefully lay Dracula
Upon a wooden stretcher.
Ann and Tonie take up the rear
And Tommie in front as master.

They follow their guides, Dwayne and Tabitha,
As very dutiful soldiers,
Finding Dracula's body not as heavy
As they had all supposed.
This is no doubt due to the joy,
Which they anticipate
Up to the roof, it'll soon be over,
Then they'll be out of this place.

Changing of the Guard

Yea, in their route up to the roof,
Only one brief stop they make.
But when they do, it is as if
A veil is ripped away.

The atmosphere is now suppressed,
As with a very bad omen,
And though the trio can't explain it,
They feel it in their bones.

Between the three, nothing is said,
But they indeed detect
That Dwayne and Tabitha is isolated
From them in all respect.

For one, they have increased the distance,
Making themselves a group,
Consisting of conversational dialogue
Of which the trio are mute.

And even though they cannot hear
Their voices or their words,
The main thing is their faces reveal
The goodness of their worth.

The main thing that they want right now
Is a supportive helping hand,
Regardless of the form it takes
To free them from this land.

However, with all due respect,
Ann will not let it go.
"I do not like this, not at all,"
She says low in her throat.

"Yo, as a whole I think that this
Indeed is a setup."
In mock surprise out of nowhere,
Tommie now exclaims, "You what?

Ann, why so critical all the time?
Even though this place is weird,
Let's make the best with what we have
Of the people helping us here."

Though this is said, even Tommie himself
Is quite a bit unsettled;
But he, like Tonie, wants to believe
No other way is better.

"Indeed, indeed, our circumstances
Are unusual at best."
This is the statement Tonie makes
When she does interject.
Oh boy, oh boy, if she had seen
The looks upon their faces
Upon her making this lame statement,
She'd do a double take.

And for the reason she missed their glares,
Tonie continues on,
"As logic suggests, the odds of all this
Is totally zero to none.

But evidently the odds are off.
Let's not be overdramatic."
Tonie tries to find the perfect word,
Then totally resigns at last.

"Well, Tabitha and Dwayne are the only ones
Who knows what's going down,
And better still they're willing to help us
And get us back to town."

Quick and nervous, Ann counters her.
"Well, who's to say for sure
It wasn't them who put us here
And used those letters for lure."

They've had enough; their rope pulled taunt.
Together both they grit teeth.
Her first name they both murmur fully,
Which halt Ann on her feet.
She shrugs her shoulders resolved and frustrated,
Having come to a dead end.
"But don't say I didn't tell you so
When you see I'm right again."

There's contentment and complacency
Etched on all their faces,
But deep inside each one of them,
There is a storm a raging.

It's mentally they're battling,
Strategically in mind,
Trying to put the facts together
Through sensible reason or rhyme.

There's definitely something amiss.
It tries to click in place;
But all the more it seems elusive,
Given the leads they trace.

Or maybe it's as Tonie said
That none of this is real.
No matter what the case may be,
Soon something has to give.

Dwayne and Tabitha motion them.
It's time for us to go.
Now this she says as they approach
The top stairs of the floor.

TRUE FACES REVEALED

The floor, it leads onto the roof
Into the great outdoors.
It's been a while since being outside.
Yes, now they're ready to go.

They had forgotten how invigorating
The open air could be
Until they step out on the roof
And breathe in very deeply.

The air isn't cold, but very cool,
Enough to wake their senses.
While in the castle, it was suffocating
As being sealed in a coffin.

The twinkling stars high up above
Do shine so radiantly bright
Against a deep and mud-black sky,
So nothing is hidden from sight.

The moon itself is bursting full
With a harsh ebb brightness to it
That combs the air with anticipation
And wet the atmosphere.

Tommie suppresses his total surprise
When they are on the roof.
He sees that Tabitha has been busy
Looking down at the proof.

There in the center of the roof,
A pentagram is painted.
Its diameter is of seven feet,
Lines perfectly arranged.

Upon interruption of their love session,
That's when she'd made her move
To complete the task she had at hand
To give them back their groove.

But Tommie does not fancy this.
Indeed, it's just the opposite.
His heart goes sore; his head does ache
To think he'd almost lost it.

Back to the details of the pentagram,
Its circumference is perfectly round,
With four-inch lines done in blood paint,
That glisten off the ground.

The odor is fresh, but the smell is off.
There's something familiar there
That tug at them like a well-drawn veil
Of which they can't quite grasp.
When all of them are on the roof
Now under the crescent sky,
They've stepped into a different world,
Which they don't recognize.

It's not just their natural surroundings
That's totally altered by far,
But even Tabitha and Dwayne as well
Have also changed their parts.

As passive helpers they are no more
But aggressive in behavior
And slowly sheds the benevolent suits
Of being heroic saviors.

Immediately and forcibly,
Dwayne takes up Tommie's position,
Quite easily displacing him
And asking no permission.

He says commandingly, "I'll take that!"
Easily brushing Tommie aside,
Practically knocking him down,
As if though swatting a fly.

And though the slightest of a touch,
Does pass between the two,
The purest of fear hits Tommie so hard,
He doesn't know what to do.
He finds himself thinking within,
His strength, it is unearthly,
And someone ought to check his manners.
But now it's not that urgent.

Tabitha performs the same scenario
Both with Ann and Tonie.
"Excuse me, girls, now I'll take that,"
Being coy and not so funny.

Ann feels the urge to lash straight out
And gives her all she has,
But her intuition steers her better
Regarding this here matter.

They ought to all retaliate
And put their two cents in.
Instead, the three instinctively
Reign in their own alliance.

They know that they are going to need
All their strength combined
To deal with what may come up next
So not to be confined.

Within the large red pentagram,
Both Dwayne and Tabitha work,
Both laboring laboriously,
But now without a word.
Meanwhile, Ann and Tonie and Tommie
Observe from a safe distance,
Very carefully taking in
All of the proceedings.

In the center of the pentagram,
There sits a large throne chair,
Backseat cushions and armrests as well,
The color of ruby-red hair.

The trimming is wood of the darkest black
That they have ever seen.
Its high gloss luster sucks up life
Beneath the moonlight's beam.

There're various colors of precious stones
Aligning the arm of the chair.
Their glittering light gives an eerie feeling
That drains life from the air.

With much more than the usual care,
They now sit Dracula upright.
His eyes are boring straight ahead
With a wild infectious smile.

The two of them, Dwayne and Tabitha,
Now move as if subservient,
As if now catering his every wish
To bring forth his fulfillment.
And of a truth this is the case
Though it is impossible.
But yet our trio accepts this fact
Way deep down in their thoughts.

They stand at length in silence retreat,
Watching with intensity,
And give much thought to everything
That's said and done indeed.

Upon completion, Dwayne and Tabitha,
Now take up their positions,
Dwayne on the right, Tab on the left,
They each stand next to him.

The manner in which they stand abreast
On either side of Dracula
Does put our trio in the mind
Of seeing a family portrait.

That large and ancient dusty book,
Which they used in the library,
Is opened wide in Tabitha's hands
For what she's now preparing.

She reads aloud; her voice is strong
That carries on the wind,
Which once was calm but now is restless
Just as her speech begins.
This wild, uncanny circumstance
By no means go unnoticed,
But more than ought it cause a stir
Amid our weary trio.

Refreshing Echo

The three of them are so unsettled.
They interlock their hands
That they might draw strength from one another.
It's Tonie, Tommie, and Ann.

They back themselves flush to the wall
Till they can go no further.
The three-feet-wide brick castle ledge
Is now a permanent barrier,

Raised from the roof's floor having height
That limit their escape.
They all together, in one fluid motion,
Perform a double take.

They dare to look over the edge of the roof
And peer into the darkness
To see below the endless ravine,
Which earlier they had crossed.

And instantly, they have a flashback,
Recalling to remembrance
The bridge which makes them ache and shiver,
Thinking of its image.

To shake the pot and make it worse,
Tabitha's voice chimes on
And fill the air with an eerie omen
With a life of its very own.

They do not understand a word
Of what is spoken out,
But all the more this garbled language
Is evil without doubt.

This is a fanfare of the worst.
That's joyous by no means.
Instead, it is a eulogy,
Rippling at the seam.

Now once again they all turn back
Simultaneously
To face their allies Dwayne and Tabitha,
Who now are adversaries.

They face off here to opposing foes,
Tonie to Dwayne, Tommie to Tab,
And there at last but not the least,
It's Ann who faces Dracula.

The wind now howls with sadness strong
As gazes quickly lock
Eye to eye and person to person,
Death stirring in the pot.
It only last for a split second,
Then suddenly is broken
By a thunderous crashing, pounding sound,
As if the floor has opened.

But this descending, pounding crash
Descends not from the sky
But rather come from down below
From the ravine's endless eye.

The sky above does have no clouds,
And so it can't be thunder.
And then the trio know the answer,
Plunging them all in wonder.

"This is the echo of the bridge
That crashed down earlier,
Now only resending back to us
To make us more alert."

In light of this new evidence,
The fact is now dispelled
That this ravine indeed is endless,
Which they thought went to hell.

In any case this golden fleece
Of distraction does them well,
Shocking them back, enlightening their minds
Of many important details.

A Time Thing

Thus, by following the outlined instructions
Of Dwayne and Tabitha,
The trio signed their own death warrants,
Which now is wreaking havoc.

They had been used so all along
And mislead to a tee.
And if they ever make it out,
Ann gets an apology.

Now all the questions in their minds
Curiosity had sown
Of Tabitha's and Dwayne's dark black eyes
Is fully now made known.

The moment of truth is in their eyes.
It cannot be denied.
Their bond with Dracula, it is there.
It is a family tie.

In unison, yea, all of them,
Yo, Tonie, Ann, and Tommie,
Their mouths drop open and eyes spread wide
At these Dracula prodigies.

What a standoff, how ironic,
Three villains stand astride
Against three loyal and faithful friends,
Who are standing side by side.

It's plain to see in this face-off
The intention of the bad.
They plan to have a dinner feast,
Whose fangs are smiling glad.

The blood-revealing lusty fangs,
Cancerous with satisfaction,
Let our heroes know this time
They are the food attraction.

It's both ironic and sad to say
As victims they remember.
At one time, it was them who chased
The bad guy and the villain.

'Twas like a dream then at that time,
Chasing the headless horseman,
But now that things have turned around,
A nightmare is in question.

The predicament that they're now in
By far is hard to fathom.
Their throats constrict with freezing air,
Their skin as hot as lanterns.
As the crashing echo dies away
Into a soft sound muffle,
It reiterates what they've known.
It was the bridge's last rustle.

They know for sure that this feedback,
It is that same roped bridge
Hitting rock bottom just only now.
With how much time now missed?

Automatically, instantly,
Does Tonie find herself
Doing some quick rough calculation
To find some sound results.

"Now, let me see how fast sound travels.
It's eleven thousand feet per second,
And we've been gone about three hours.
That's definitely is some distance.

Now, if I do the math correctly
And round it out about
111,880,000 feet.
Which is how many miles?

That's 21,190
Of minimum miles at least.
Oh boy! That is a very long drop.
That ravine is very deep."
With all that is going on right now,
Just leave it to dear Tonie
To focus on a thing like this,
For what more could go wrong?

THE O'CASTLE CHORALE

Dracula then stands to his feet,
Now tall, erect, and straight,
And flowing evenly in the wind,
His jet-black silver-lined cape.

In perfect union with Tab and Dwayne,
He takes a slow step forward.
No need to rush nor hurry up,
Time is at their disposal.

The trio's backs are against the wall.
There's nowhere else to go.
Their only exit blocked by vampires,
No way to reach the door.

Another shocking and shattering thought,
Flash quick through Tommie's mind.
He finally solves that nagging taunt
From an earlier point in time.

He looks down at the pentagram,
Painted freshly on the roof.
Its glistening color and copper smell
Give him his needed proof.

Something ignites deep down inside,
And now he does remember.
He knows for sure the origin of
The paint that Tab have rendered.

On shaky legs with trembling voice,
Tommie nudges his companions
To look down at the painted symbols
On which the moon now shines.

He quietly says in a raspy voice,
"Remember the centaur lady?"
With that they all recall at once
That shrill scream heard to date.

At midnight, they remember when
They stood there in the library.
It had not been a shrieking bat
As Dwayne had surely said.

It reasoned out and made much sense
Why the lady looked so real.
Bound and gagged in the centaur's arms,
She was the very real deal.

It is her blood that now does coat
The symbols on the roof,
Shining brightly in the moonlight,
Here staged for evil use.
My God! My God! What terrible fate
Had this poor girl gone through.
They do not wish to know at all,
For they may be soon too.

With all the bloody facts laid out,
One question do they table.
"How do we avoid these vampires' clutches
And make our great escape?"

They wrestle with this great dilemma
Collectively as one,
Though there aren't any audible sounds
That from their mouths do come.

And even in the light of this,
Of all that have so happened,
They even still now find it hard
To let go and accept this.

THE DARE

But one thing they do know for sure,
The one means of escape
Is to the door and down the stairs
And through the castle's gates.

But as it stands, this will not happen
Lest there's a big surprise.
That's when Tonie, Ann, and Tommie
Gaze in the others' eyes.

They speculate how to get pass
Beyond these blood-sucking vultures,
And though the odds are not too good,
A prayer rest at the altar.

As justice is it may be so
That one of them might make it
If they make a loud commotion,
Along with a great ruckus.

So if they all dash for the door
And rush at the same time,
There is a good chance one of them
Might make it on a dime.

The set of three jet boring black eyes
That's taunt with satisfaction,
Does tease them with an arrogance
To go ahead and try it!

Between Ann and Tonie, along with Tommie,
No words are necessary.
They merely gaze back at one another
With clear intent available.

They turn their gaze back to the door.
It's either now or never,
And with high tension between these gangs,
Something must unravel.

At this moment, it's will against will
And evil against the good,
As well as the strong against the weak,
Like metal against strong wood.

You're put in mind of the western days,
Seeing a frontier shoot-out,
Where everyone is set on edge
To see who wins the fight.

Hey, will the law-abiding sheriff
Be triumphant in the end?
Or will it be the rule-breaking robbers
That make the final mend?
Intensity soars in the atmosphere.
The string is about to snap.
Everything has now come to a head
As everyone takes a breath.

Tonie, with Ann and Tommie, exhales
And dashes three steps ahead.
Pure desperation fuels their steps,
Ignoring all their dread.

They go for all that they do know.
There is no turning back.
They cannot stop this downward spiral,
So instead they change the track.

Despite their speed and super strength,
Our villains are not prepared
To handle what comes at them next.
There's nothing to compare.

They can but only stand completely
Motionless on the spot,
Gaping and gagging with lagging tongues
With eyes wide in their sockets.

Dracula with Dwayne and Tabitha too
Are trying to comprehend.
They're at a loss, confused completely,
And trying to come to terms.
There is no reason they can see
How they have missed their prey.
How could they have slipped through their fingers
And totally gotten away?

This is one night, a candid sight,
Where bones which are so dry
Will thus be joined by thirsty veins,
Which too have missed their bite.

THE GREAT ESCAPE

Yea, this is how the great escape
For Tonie, Ann, and Tommie
Went down when they faced off the vampires
And made them look like dummies.

Full steam ahead moved Tonie, Ann, and Tommie,
Straight toward the exit door.
Directly standing in their path
Did stand the evil trio.

The gangs move forward with every step
On each opposing team,
The vampires with their arms outstretched
As welcoming king and queen.

Their invitation is all too clear.
Delight dances in their eyes
To savor the sweet and rosy liquid
On which all life does thrive.

It's seen as well upon their lips
Their parched and thirsty grins,
Reveling in the bliss of it all
For a feast to soon begin.

But strange enough, the only thing
That meet when they collide
Is flowing air when the Dracula gang
Embrace them for a bite.

This is ironic, the second time
That this indeed has happened.
It seems these youngsters have a knack
To make things take a nap.

And as for Dracula and both his siblings,
Their feast is sore denied.
Neither flesh for food nor blood for drink
Will be served up tonight.

Yea, creatures of the night they are,
Both strong and versatile too
And virtually invulnerable,
Yet something went askew.

THE DESCENT

For as fast as our famous trio
Made for the exit door,
They, on their third step, simultaneously
Made a sudden detour.

Letting go of one another's hands,
They made an about-face.
Not even slowing down their motion,
This sounds familiar I'll say.

Then once more joining hands again,
They take three dashing steps.
Heading in the opposite direction,
The bad guys they have left.

Their powder steps do thrust them up,
Then out into the open.
They're over the ledge of the castle's roof
And away from the bad folks.

'Tis their escape from these vampires
To be free of their clutches.
It may not seem a wise decision,
But this is their best choice.

Given a choice of tangling with
Those blood carved sucking vampires,
They'd rather take their chance by far
With a death-dive over the side.

So with that said, their slogan goes
Up, up, up and away,
Or to be precise in their case,
Down, down, down to the grave.

Their actions were so unified
And as natural as to wit.
It was as if it was pre-written
And played out in a script.

They hardly can believe themselves,
What they have all just done.
Have they become now so dislodged
From reality of the normal?

For they have done a crazy thing
And sealed their own death-fate
By dividing off the castle's roof
That can but end one way.

But hey, hey, hey, they had to do,
Yea, that which serves them best,
And given the choice to do it again,
The same would come to rest.
The first few seconds of their ascent
Into the open sky,
They float with the feeling of ecstasy,
Each moment going higher and higher.

The air is warm and cool about them,
And then reality hits.
They fall with fingers wrapped about them,
The feel of a ton of bricks.

The weightlessness they felt before
Is gone as they now plummet
While moving hard so very fast
Down to their death-drop dungeon.

But all too well before their drop,
They never will forget
The slack-jaw look upon these faces,
Expressions to be missed.

The moonlight glowed like white sapphires
Upon the vampires' faces,
Trying to figure out what happened
While all stood there quite dazed.

Their expressions are oh quite priceless
And worth all the trouble,
Which our trio have been put through.
This payback to them is double.
The stale air rushes past their bodies
Through every anatomy's contour,
Creating a whistling stream of air,
Sounding like a jet for sure.

Their increasing sound increases in speed
As they descend below.
The sound is deafening in their ears
Till they can hear no more.

Profusely perspiring are their bodies
So that they can't discern
As to whether they are hot or cold,
In a freezer or a furnace.

There is only a numbing sensation
Squeezing them inside out.
The only thing that they can see
Is the darkness swirling about.

The air's so dense that screaming is useless.
It does not pay at all.
They cannot breathe either in nor out
Within these darkened walls.

They gradually become light-headed
And start to register colors,
Bright and vivid in assorted details
In flickering patterns of sort.
It is completely indeterminable,
The perception that is used,
The physical eyes or the mental mind
That bring these things in view.

But this does not make any difference
As one thing is for sure.
Their whole lives pass right before them.
For them there is no cure.

Thus, with the viewing of these events,
All else is irrelevant.
There's no more barriers to what is norm,
Entering another realm.

Faster and deeper are they drawn
Into the sucking black void.
Panic stabs their hearts with anticipation,
Embracing their final reward.

Ironically fast, life comes at them.
The end as well does that,
For it is sudden without a warning,
Right through the blackness, *whack!*

Is That It?

Now everything becomes all black.
It's nothing here at all.
No pain, no fear, happiness nor tears,
Just one black solid wall.

At the Party Door

Whack. Whack! Whack!

Thunder crackles in the sky above
And shake the heaven as well.
The rattling ground drown out the sound
That's made by the doorbell.

So once again there is a whack,
A ruckus at the door
As Tonie and Ann and Tommie stand
Amid the noise and roar.

Indeed, they're filled with anticipation,
Excited they have arrived,
To partake in the Halloween party
To which they've been invited.

While at the door waiting with patience,
Tommie looks down at his watch
To make sure that they are on time
For when the party starts.

He finds that they are in the green.
All systems are a go,
But then he does a double take
To verify the show.
It's not just him as he looks down
And gazes upon his watch.
The bubble crystal of his watch
Is cracked in certain spots.

He can't recall how this did happen
But find it very odd,
For there is nothing that they did
To bring about this cause.

Between them all, there is a blanket,
An absentee in place.
There's something that they cannot grasp
To bring back to their case.

Though it is not spoken out loud.
It's something they do know.
They can remember leaving home
And stopping at their doors.

They do remember that they entered
Into the church courtyard.
They crossed the bridge to the other side
Then all become a fog.

And from that moment until now,
Everything's a misty dream,
Where they now stand upon the porch
With a hush-hush in between.
Each know that something strange did happen,
Unusual to them all,
But had it been a dream or hoax?
Or had it happened at all?

Their stomachs feel like butterflies
That are buzzing all around
While moving fast at lightning speed,
Then slammed against the ground.

They do indeed just vaguely remember
Getting lost out in the woods
Only to meet with ghouls and goblins,
Who were up to no good.

And finally along the line,
They do recall somehow
That near the end they bit the dust,
Which brings them unto now.

Again they think unto themselves
In quiet and silent thoughts.
That none of this makes any sense.
It doesn't add up at all.

Independently, yet all together,
They simultaneously check
Their bodies for scars, abrasions, and cuts
From down below the neck.
Despite all this, there is no sign
Out of the ordinary
To even suggest that they've experienced
Something quite extraordinary.

Their bodies are fine, in good condition,
In spite of all their jitters.
Why should it not be even so
When nothing happened really?

And all together with a sigh,
They let out a big breath,
Relieved to know it was a dream
And really nothing else.

INTO THE PARTY

The door creaks open and swings in wide;
And spewing out from its edges
Are curling whiff of white puff vapor,
Which makes them all feel edgy.

To top this off when they look up,
They're startled to the max
To see the doorman at the entrance
Whose look defies the mask.

They're looking at a growling werewolf,
Whose smile is quite contagious,
Who cordially now motions them in,
Noting their invitations.

Quickly they regain their posture
And pull it back together.
Forgetting this is a Halloween party,
The costume is what matters.

This tall thin guy wearing the costume,
He looks and sounds so real.
They'd nearly forgot why they're here
So not to run in fear.

Momentarily a bit still frightened,
They freeze there in their tracks
Until the spell is broken by
The thunder that goes crack!

Then childishly they move inside
Into the house for safety
Against the storm that's coming on
That's threatening to now break.

For now, the moon is bright and full
Above high in the sky.
It feels as if it's shooting threats
With bright orb beams of light.

Of course they know that it is silly
That they should feel at odds,
Like everything is out to get them
To leap out from the dark.

But at the moment these sensations
Are just the way they feel.
They cannot change or alter this.
It's all to them so real.

THE PARTY HOUSE

They buckle down and tell themselves
Indeed, things will get better.
They've made it to the Halloween party,
And that is all that matters.

Because they're here with the big wig,
They want to fit right in.
Prestige and glory can be achieved
Of which they plan to win.

"So while we're here, let's do our part
And present ourselves as smart,
And since we have these invitations,
We're sure it's in the cards."

This being their first and major party,
They want to get it right,
So with all grace and proper poise,
They causally move inside.

But Lord almighty and gracious alive,
They cannot hold it in,
Their eyes now widen in great amazement
When they see what's within.

This haunted house is otherworldly.
How can it be described?
It looks and feels as if they have
Entered another time.

The authenticity is far beyond
The mere shake of the hand
But looks as if it's totally displaced,
Moved from a time span.

The furnishings are detail-exquisite
Directly from the pages
Of the late-eighteenth-century era,
Not a single item misplaced.

The elegant touch of French provincial,
Aside the artistry,
Does set the tone above all board
To a level of ecstasy.

Even the curtains so masterfully done
Glide down like silken screens
That makes the place seem oh surreal,
Bubbled in its own realm,

Which are adorned with ribbons and bonnets
And laced with bows astride,
Though fresh and new and neatly hung,
They're caked with dust quite high.
This by no means degrades the scene
But all the more does add
A vintage and a character,
An appeal that isn't bad.

There is a good; there is a bad
Within this place withal.
They only need to focus themselves
And keep the narrow walk.

This whole place is a dream withal,
A world of fantasy
That woos the eyes and warms the heart
To join the revelry.

They look about, being struck with awe,
With prospect of a life
That would make them an intricate part
Of this elite socialite.

If they became part of this group,
There is no doubt at all
They would excel at everything
That beckon at their call.

Indeed, indeed, this would be great.
Beyond their wildest dreams,
They will at last achieve their goal
And have the highest esteem.
But even as they think on this,
A grave thought does arise.
To have this kind of spoiled lifestyle,
What is the ultimate price?

And even more would they so dare
To make such sacrifice
To forfeit all that they now have
Down to their very lives?

Their edginess and nervousness,
It's only natural.
In a place anew and both unknown,
It's hard to be so casual.

THE DECISION

Now under these strange circumstances
With feelings that are mixed,
They take the time to gather themselves
And hold together their wits.

So for the moment, none do speak
To one another or others
But take this time for indigestion
Of what they have discovered.

Their first step is to browse around
Curiously as a group,
Absorbing all their surroundings,
Along with the guests too.

It is a sight beyond belief.
The costumes of the guests,
They are so real and so lifelike.
No one would ever guess.

And though they are but only props
Displayed to look the best,
The trio's heartbeat race with speed,
Refusing to find rest.

And as concerning the excitement,
This society now shows
There are no limits or unscaled walls,
Nor are there any tight sealed doors
To bar the wonder of what they have
That sparkles, shines, and glows.

Our trio now see perfectly well.
Indeed, this organization
Do not hold back in anything
In their grand presentation.

This place itself does emanate
Wealth, prestige, and power
Perfectly aired with the illusion
That sets it in the clouds.

But yet and still it permeates
In smell and touch alike,
A realness which do dazzle the senses
Beyond all common surprise.

This house's decorum alone is staged
To win a Noble Prize
As seen upon Ann's glowing face,
Fire sparkling in her eyes.

They loosen up as time passes by
But stay a little on edge,
As though they're holding back a part
Just for emergency case.

All of them are totally amazed,
Especially dear Ann,
As they survey the entire charade
Of the Halloween-dressed band.

Seems every ghoul they can imagine
Do seem to be here now,
Comprising this here Halloween party
And doing it with a wow.

The rooms are quite elaborate
With artifacts and paintings
Of statues, weapons, books, and instruments
Frightful, intriguing, enchanting.

Ann's interest is the one peaked most;
Thus, she is first to speak.
"Indeed, this place is unbelievable.
Do you not all agree?"

Tommie agrees with a low whistle,
"You bet your bottom it is.
With all this stuff here lying around,
It hardly can be real."
"Well, normally I would concur"
Is Tonie's quick response.
"But from my observation here,
I have to be forthcoming.

Here in conclusion of our surroundings,
It is difficult to conceive
That such display of this great wealth
Is done in modesty

The remnants of these artifacts..."
But this is where she stops
Upon her seeing her comrades' faces
With slack jaws and dropped mouths.

Then clearing her throat, she starts again
So they can understand
And flatly state, "I apologize.
This place is open and frank."

"Oh my! What are you trying to say?"
Asks Ann with much excitement.
Yea, at this point, seen in Ann's eyes
Is a shining light that glints.

It's Tommie who does answer Ann
With a question of his own.
"You mean to say all this is real,
And none of it is phony?"
Of Tommie's reference, there's many items
To which he does refer,
Golden napkins and silverware,
Studded with diamonds and pearls,

Statues of gold, silver, and brass,
And other precious metals,
Paintings and portraits artfully done
By artists known as masters,

Memorial pieces from famous shrines,
Emblazoned furnishings' artworks.
And these are just the material things,
Not counting the other perks.

The tiny twinkle in Ann's eyes
Has now become a blaze;
Then together, Tonie and Tommie say,
"Ann, please calm down your crave!

Decision Made

Let's keep our minds in proper perspective
The purpose of why we're here,
Our goal is to get in with them,
Becoming close-knit peers.

So if we play our cards correctly,
We'll be part of the crowd,
Then all our needs and dreams and wants
Will make us strong and proud.

Then Tonie adds, "We are together,
No matter what comes our way."
Next Tommie says, "That being the case,
Then everything looks okay."

Then from a tray, he takes a goblet,
Holding it casually.
"We fit in with the people here,"
He says this avidly.

"Well, we will see," Tonie retorts,
Her voice a little bit shaky.
The others notice, especially Ann,
Whose blaze now starts to fade.

The gleam resides still in Ann's eyes,
But now it dims a little.
And her baby blue eyes start to cloud
To a hazel color that's brittle.

So then she asks, "What is it, Tonie?"
Who answers in reply.
"Nothing," she responds oh so solemn,
Offering a very weak smile.

Then shaking her head just a little.
"I'm merely thinking too hard.
Let's just enjoy ourselves at length
And get on with the party."

But Tommie knows her all too well,
Despite what she does say.
There's something here more to the eye
Than what they can assay.

He also knows that none of them
Desire to talk about it,
But inside he knows that he must
Confront it now aloud.

The best way to get good results
Is to deal with it directly,
And now he feels such is the case
And will do so correctly.
Being very subtle, Tommie asks,
"Tonie, are you okay?
And if you do not mind at all,
What is the time of day?"

This does the trick maybe all too well
As Tonie looks at her watch,
For in that moment Tommie sees
A flicker of some shock.

It's almost imperceptible,
But Tommie gets a glance
To see her brown-colored pecan eyes
Withdraw back from that trance.

Though she recovers full and quickly,
Tommie sees before it's gone
That sense of "Did it really happen,
Or am I all alone?"

Her voice is strained as she speaks out
And looking down as well.
"It seems somehow my watch was damaged.
Just when I cannot tell."

Her eyes are fixed; she does not move.
It's then Ann takes the cue.
Happily giving her assistance,
She comes to the rescue.
And with a smile, "Well, that's no problem,"
Until she too looks down.
And that is when her smile is turned
Into a worried frown.

They all stand frozen, huddled together,
The one, two, three of them,
Looking at their broken crystals
Around their watches' rims.

Their arms extended toward one another,
As if they're making a pact,
They see the designs on each watch
Of which are all exact.

Not only that but they have stopped
And ceased to keep the time.
Right down unto the second hand,
They've stopped on the same dime.

And at this sight, they all go cold.
It's Ann who breaks the code.
"This has to be a coincidence,"
She says in doubtful hope.

Then Tommie counters with cold sarcasm,
"Coincidence, yeah, right."
And then it's Tonie's time to speak.
Her throat is very tight.

Her voice is cool and also menacing.
"I do believe this so.
We must now extricate ourselves.
Indeed, we now must go.

It is indeed to our best interest
To find the nearest exit
And quickly and as quietly
Get off these premises.

I mean like expeditiously,"
Tonie reiterates.
Says Tommie, "If you mean let's book,
Then I am in the race."

Ann shakes her head quite vigorously,
Agreeing with the plan.
"But we must be so very careful,"
Says Tonie, looking at Ann.

With this disturbing discovery,
Tommie looks down at his cup,
Discretely discards the bright-red liquid.
There is no bottom-up.

At this moment, they're all self-conscious
About themselves at large.
They feel as if every eye in house
Is staring them down hard.
"Yes, as of now we must act natural
And keep down all suspicions
And make our way out of this place.
Now this is our sole mission."

It's Exit Time

Their outer mannerism, mild and pleasant,
Yet inside's a different story
As they try to keep it all together
While heading toward the door.

In after thought Tommie gives a sigh
Of what might just have been,
A most grave error if he had sipped
And tasted that red gin.

In hush-hush tones among themselves,
They speak in low conversation
But show themselves to everyone else
Alive with liberation.

They show excitement for the party,
Methodically moving about,
Making their way back to the door
So that they can get out.

In this regard their hopes are high
As they move closer now,
Closing the distance with each moment,
For soon they will be out.

In bits and pieces, they listened to
Their recount to one another
Regarding their strange nightmare visions,
Which they find most disturbing.

Between these three, what seems to be
Is not so easily received,
For Tonie's logic tells them so
That such things cannot be.

"I know in fact that none of this
Can thus befall us all,
And for the very sake of it,
It's all just like a fog.

You can see it. You can feel it,
But as for all the rest,
When you try and grab to hold it,
It slips right through your grasp."

Now Tonie continues to reason it out,
"Taken from a logical point,
There's no disputing certain facts
Of which we can confront.

For instance, if we did incur
The things we think we did,
It surely would have left some mark
That's concrete and quite solid.
Yes, definitely, oh, there would be
Something that would so state
The solidarity of all this.
Do this not sound okay?"

And with her smile, this does the trick
To assure them with some comfort,
Which urges them to make the move
To face the facts upfront.

And so they look one another over
For abrasions, cuts, or marks
That would've appeared upon them all
If such events were wrought.

Visible relief washes over them
As no evidence is found,
Outside their normal body marks
That's always been around.

But still there is uneasiness
Of which they cannot shake,
Which probably will not disappear
Until they leave this place.

In light of what they'd hoped to gain
From this great Halloween party,
It seems the table has changed the cards
From ace to bloody hearts.
All the fun and wild excitement
For which they had come for
Has turned out to be ghastly tricks,
Which they cannot afford.

At least there is one consolation,
Which is when they awake.
They'll find that this was only a dream,
A very bad, ill mistake.

And with this thought they have already
Begun to feel much better
And even break out into smiles,
Knowing none of this does matter.

They're thinking how just silly they are,
Acting like little children,
Believing in all those old folktales
Of witches, ghosts, and goblins.

With genuine smiles among themselves,
They do put on display,
Pondering just how silly they are
Showing forth such child behavior.

Now do foretell, oh, is it not
The very time in their lives
That they should act as grown adults,
Sensible without the jive?
After a deep long breath, they then exhale,
Feeling their jolly old selves
Now back to normal, all nonsense forgotten.
They're feeling quite good and swell.

Only minutes away and soon they'll be
On the other side of the door,
Rolling with laughter at one another
And feeling no remorse.

Detention Starts

They approach the door and suddenly
They all come to a halt.
Tonie and Tommie are the first
To simultaneously stop,

The two of them at the same time
By two events are tipped.
That simultaneously happens as well,
Which now detours their trip.

The first is when they see dear Ann.
Her face goes white as snow.
That chokes off all her merriment;
Instead, it's fear that shows.

The catalyst which does bring this on
Is a voice that's so familiar
From a hostess who's approaching them,
Who's sweet and smooth as silk.

At the very sound of this girl's voice,
Their hearts do skip a beat.
Their mouths go dry and muscles bunch,
As if they're hit from electricity.

Now all their hopes do suddenly plummet,
Cast far, far, far away
As mental harmony and psychic synch
Do open their mouths to say,

"That's Tabitha. Indeed, it is.
How can that even be?"
In this same instance, there is no time,
Reality, nor sanity.

Instantly for Tonie, Ann, and Tommie,
Yea, there is only nothingness.
They can't discern the hours or days
Nor the seconds nor the minutes.

They do not know; they do not care.
But collectively they stand,
Drawing on everything inside them,
Fending off never, never land.

Bracing one another, supporting one another,
They stand together as one,
Physically holding one another's hand
With extension far beyond.

Yea, this entwining, it now reaches
To their very existence,
Encompassing not just merely the body
But also soul and spirit.
It's only through this bond of care,
Their deep concern for each
That keep them holding on to life
To thwart oblivion's deep.

They have the drive; they are determined.
They will not fold or snap.
They will survive and hold on tight,
Avoiding this terrible trap.

"Hello, hello, oh, there you are."
The hostess's voice does boom.
Authoritative yet soft and kind,
It sweeps them like a broom.

It holds a threat, and that's for sure
Yet subtle as can be.
It seems as if the fingers of fate
Have turned against these three.

Upon Ann's surprised and horrific reaction
Of their hostess's sudden appearance,
The others turn, step to her side,
Moving together in unison.

They're at her side in an instant,
Not leaving her alone
To face the onslaught of their assailant,
No matter what may come.

The Initiation Starts

It is indeed but a few seconds
Yet seems like it's forever
As they look upon their new hostess
To find out who's the better.

They struggle deep within themselves
With staggering strength and stamina
To stay composed, not lose control,
Knowing exactly what will happen.

They're tense and ready to combat
When recognition do set in.
When Tabitha remembers them,
They'll fight unto the end.

A very big scene played out right here
In the middle of the party.
Heads will roll and bodies will fly,
And there goes their sorority.

To their surprise, there is no scene.
There is no fright or brawl.
They cannot fathom what is happening.
It makes no sense at all.

Instead, the lady covers her breasts,
Crisscrossing both her hands,
And in her eyes is genuine start
As she makes it quite plain.

"I am so sorry I frightened you.
Accept my apology."
Their gazes lock with her dark eyes,
So rounded perfectly.

So captivating is her gaze.
They visibly relax
And see the posture in her as well,
Also go down like that.

"Dear Ann," she says, "are you all right?
Would you like to sit down?"
At this Ann only shakes her head,
Keeping at bay her frown.

In all their heads and going off wildly,
Alarming bells do ring.
There's something here that isn't right,
There's something here that's mean.

Just like a wasp's quick deadly sting,
Which hurts and is unseen,
Our dear trio try to make out
What's happening on the scene.
The hostess catches their weary looks
As seen upon their faces
And says, "Of course. I know your names.
It's written on your name plates.

Indeed, you are our honored guests
By special invitation,
Or otherwise it is for sure,
You wouldn't be in this place.

I am your hostess...here to serve
To welcome you with smiles."
And with this explanation given,
They all let out a sigh.

But even still with all this said,
Whether paranoid or not,
They can't completely regard this as
A fluke as they would like.

And though their hostess is just that,
A young teen eager to serve,
She has a very uncanny resemblance
Of the bad blood-sucking girl.

The one that haunts the trio's nightmare,
Which they all share together,
A common thread that can't be broken,
Despite the stormy weather.
They're broken from their revelry,
Also their willies as well,
By the bright and cheerful disarming smile
Of the young lady who does tell.

"Oh, we're so glad that we found you.
It is almost that time
For your great initiation
Of which will be divine.

Your presentation is our privilege
As our dear guests tonight,
So if you would just follow us,
Everything will be alright.

The best of our festivities
Will be in the main hall.
It's there that you will get to meet
The whole crew of us all."

As she politely moves pass them
To lead them on their way,
There is a moment brief in time
That Tommie goes astray.

Her intoxicating perfume of fragrance,
Its smell regurgitates
Hidden feelings and strange emotions
That are tucked down deep away.
For his reaction to this hostess
Is very unsettling to him,
And oddly enough he also finds,
It is also familiar.

Thinking silently to himself,
She smells so wonderful.
Also included in the package,
She is a beautiful woman!

But just as fast as this thought comes,
It quickly fades away,
As if it is a pesky gnat
That's very quickly negated.

And given now their situation,
They can but follow suit,
Proceeded by their very kind hostess
But wishing they didn't have to.

Her disposition is gracious and kind,
A scene they will not make,
But they're not sure that what they're doing
Will show the light of day.

For the further that they move away,
More distanced from the door,
They feel they're losing their life raft
With nowhere else to go.
Again are they being paranoid,
Or are they just being cautious?
Considering all that they've been through,
Are they reasoning as they ought?

Still they're trying to wrap their minds
Around what is for real.
And so whatever their reasoning is,
It is a packaged deal.

Each step they make seem to dictate
A loss of lingering hope.
But as they move along they find
Things changes and unfold.

THE WELCOMING COMMITTEE

They find despair is not complete
As they thus move along
And consciously become aware
Of what is going on.

Among the crowd and group of people
Are applause and cheering shouts,
And this onslaught of mass approval,
It's them it's all about.

Good natured fellowship is seen
Among all these kind folks,
Who root for them with such realness
Emotion makes them choke.

Their costumes are so imaginably real.
Consisting of every kind
Of creatures spawned on Halloween,
It really blows the mind.

If they had only this to look at
To coast themselves ahead,
They would be petrified with fear,
As if among the dead.

But fueled by roars of strong support
Upon them from the crowd,
This pump them forward with heads held high
And lifted hearts of pride.

The gloom is gone; and they feel good,
Tommie, Ann, and Tonie
As they are led by the young hostess,
Also with her companion.

And with her young male counterpart,
Who tails them from the rear,
Tabitha leads our young trio
Through a crowd of merry cheers.

The crowd does open, parting a path
As they walk down the hall
That's long with a ceiling that's very high
Leading up to doors quite tall.

Within a few expanding minutes,
To the double doors they come.
Giants, they are of fresh smelling elm,
Very beautiful in sum.

Their surfaces are highly polished
To a fine and glossy shine,
All the hardware of gold and silver,
Detailed and intricate designs.
All of this is so breathtaking,
Exciting to a climax.
Their minds are racing with wild thoughts,
Not sure that they can take it.

The girl now motions at this point
With one of her smooth hands
To stop a distance from the door
As she now takes command.

She gestures with her other hand
Unto the male hostess,
Who comes and stands next to her side,
Where he can now be noticed.

As each of them take up position
Before the double doors,
It strikes a chord through our trio,
Not noticing him before.

But when they see these two together,
They do a double take,
The same thing going through each one's head,
"Identical twins, oh great."

Them being twins is not disturbing;
Instead, it's what it does.
It stirs up memories scary at heart
That cause their heads to buzz.
To them the twins offer genuine smiles
Before they open the doors.
"Congratulations! It's all for you.
Everything is now in order."

THE THREE PRISONERS

And then they push the doors wide open
And what a sight to see.
The light alone spewing from the room
Is awesome to unbelief.

Before them there's a huge parlor dome
Of magnificent conception
With different shapes and various colors
All dancing in odd patterns.

The vaulted ceiling high above
Extends at least two stories
With magnificent crystal chandeliers
That glisten with bright glory.

The reflective prism light of it
Gives off an eerie feel,
Combined with its octagonal shape
From which many doors do spill.

Again the furnishings of this room
Is magnificent at the least,
Filled with statues, paintings, and vases,
Antiques and nameless treasuries.

But all of this is small intrigue
Compared to what's ahead,
Where at the center of the room
To where they are being lead.

There in the middle of the room
Is sitting a giant cake.
So big that they can only stand
And gawk, being so amazed.

And at the sight, their legs go weak,
Trying hard just to believe
That all of this is done for them,
Who are the special three.

In front of them and facing the cake,
Three chairs are placed astride,
Just beyond the doorway entrance
From whence they stepped inside.

Three large beautiful red oak chairs
With red leather seats and arms
Are facing the cake prepared for them,
Who are the guests of honor.

Complacently they take their seats,
All dreamy and quite dazed,
No longer plagued of being afraid
With this wonderful grand display.
On Tommie's right is where Ann sits,
And Tonie is to his left.
Though much is going on round about them,
They're mostly unaware.

The other guests have filed themselves
Into this one main chamber,
Taking position along the walls
Like one big happy gang.

Of course, this gathering puts them in mind
Of a happy birthday party,
Which makes them glad they were invited
With privileges to start.

They have the advantage of sitting down;
Otherwise, this wouldn't work
As they are overcome with numbness
That's pulsing through their nerves.

Each in their way relaxes so
That they may get a grip
To understand what's really happening
Or if they should have fear.

And then they hear it and do not like it,
A total nothingness.
The rustling, the cheering, the shouting, the hooting,
It all comes to a rest.
A strong foreboding settle on them
And shock their senses awake,
Their smell's acute, their hearing is too,
Now everything is in place.

A certain aroma now saturates
Their nostrils to the max.
They know it's coming from the cake
And smells of pumpkin pie.

This is confusing; their equilibrium
Is completely thrown off balance.
Bearings are wrong, things out of sort,
There is something-to-matter.

It starts to sink in very slowly.
They've been here once before,
Like a long-dried sponge absorbing liquid,
It's surely time to go.

With this knowledge, their hearts now race
And seems to know no bounds.
Their breaths are quick and hard and labored.
They cannot make a sound.

The blood now running through their veins
Feel very cool and clammy.
They've heard this tune many times before.
It's time their feet start slamming.
They do not have to say a thing
Nor verbalize their thoughts.
They're linked together more ways than one.
Yea, this does happen often.

From their chairs they rise in unison
And head back through those doors.
Their decision final, they're leaving this party.
It's time for them to go.

There's no regrets; there's nothing wrong
With this scenario,
Except nothing happen when they rise
They're still glued to the floor.

Hey! What the heck! Tommie yelps aloud,
Breaking the stillborn silence.
His voice is now filled with despair,
As well as shaking violence.

He looks down at his arms to see
They're firmly tied down tight,
Secured unto the chair's armrests
Like Tonie's and Ann's aside.

Ann whispers in a moan, "Oh no."
Her voice is very low
Yet echoes like a cannonball,
Exploding in the snow.
Tonie is about to say some words
But swallows back her voice,
Upon thus hearing an echoed response
To Ann's weak whimpering retort.

"Oh yes," responds a feminine voice
That's cool and very suggestive.
There's satisfaction to its quality,
Aligned with severe threatening.

What's most unsettling to them all
Is the recognition.
Their skin breaks out in cold chill sweat,
Though the room is not chilled.

Collectively as if one being,
Their minds replay the past
Of their last hours occurring events,
Each sealed to the same tasks.

There is no way they can explain
How this can even be?
They are confused and totally lost,
For words they cannot speak.

They look up from their prison chairs.
Their faces etched with fear.
There's also shock and full surprise
With slack jaws wet with tears.
For looking down with devious smiles,
The twin hosts catch their eyes.
It's Dwayne and Tabitha at their sides,
Which cannot be denied.

The expression glued upon their faces,
It tells them everything
That what they thought they saw and heard
Was real and not a dream.

Their stomachs twist with knotted pain
As certainty sets in.
They shake their heads in denial defiance
And hope against hope to win.

Deny the truth but even still,
It can't be obliterated.
The truth remains when all else fails
Even on a faulty scale.

The Count's Revenge

Their present surroundings solidify.
There is no other course
Than for their conscience to accept
What now is in the works.

The smells, the sounds of hissing growls,
Gurgling, grunts, squeaks, and squeals,
These aberrations of costumes textures
Are undeniably very real.

There is no party as they supposed,
At least no costume ball.
What they see here is what they get,
The atrocity and all.

To keep some sense of dignity
Before their final demise,
They close their mouths and stop their drooling
And plaster on a smile.

There's a glint of anger in their eyes
While turning their gaze away
To leave their captors in the dark
And look ahead instead.

Here with their sight now redirected,
The situation's worse,
Having so directed their attention back
Where the pumpkin cake is perched.

There standing beside the giant cake,
A dubious figure stands
That chills their skin and heats their blood
To run hot in their veins.

Here posing like a game show host,
Presenting the main prize,
Is Dracula, clad all in black
With piercing black coal eyes.

All three of them make eye contact.
All things to them are clear.
Regardless of what happens now,
They can't give in to fear.

Dracula grins with great triumph
And sweeps his arms out wide,
Majestically commanding them
To look at what is nigh.

It's then that Dracula clears his throat.
This gesture has effect.
The entire room falls into silence
Unto a total rest.
So as he wishes, he has the floor.
His voice is recognizable,
As portrayed on late horror movies
The accent of Transylvania.

They are however quite aware
That this is not a movie.
Indeed, they are the main attraction
And do not find this groovy.

His voice is cold, harsh, and demanding,
Authority in his gestures.
Combining these, he easily wills
The youth of life itself.

There's magnetism in the air.
They sense and feel his presence,
A black draped blanket draining them
Of all their hope and strength.

Their vitality is being drained.
They know this but not how.
His vampirism is in the air
And strong like a powwow!

"Ah, welcome, ladies and gentleman,
Back to your rightful place.
We've missed you all so terribly.
We love you for your taste."
The gruesome effect of his very words
Nearly cause their bones to shatter,
Especially with its suggestive content,
Which hangs there in the air.

"We went out the way at your expense
To accommodate you all,
But as for your hospitality,
It seems you've dropped the ball."

After Dracula's speech, he stares them down,
First Tonie then onto Tommie.
Last is Ann where he lingers a bit,
Gazing a little bit longer.

This makes Ann very uncomfortable.
Did he just smack his lips?
Given their present situation,
Her stomach does a flip.

He pauses, and then waits patiently,
As if they should respond,
And if this is what he expects,
The answer he gets is none.

They are now scared out of their wits.
No strength is left in them.
It's taking everything inside
To breath and inhale in.
Besides this too, there is also
A knowing and foreboding,
A churning deep inside of them,
A déjà vu for showing.

A kind of been-there-done-that thing
Is what they are in now.
Nothing short of a miracle
Can make them safe and sound.

A miracle is just what they need.
This is their only way,
So now like never in their lives,
They do sincerely pray.

They are indeed praying very hard
So that it makes a difference.
They've definitely stepped up their game
By touching the other realm.

They would to sweat water down their face.
'Twould be a reprimand;
But they instead sit motionless,
Awaiting the end at hand.

Then Dracula moves as if sensing this
And speaks with a welcoming smile,
"Let's proceed with the ceremony
And with your big surprise.
When we last met our departure was...
Let's just say quite surprising.
But given that, I do believe
All things will head to light."

Their breaths do catch within their throats
All simultaneously
When Dracula stresses the word *head*,
Sending horror through all three.

Pumpkin Surprise

Now, things now have gone from bad to worse.
They know this without doubt
And wish that they could move a bit
To let some tension out.

But as it is they're frozen solid
And gripped from fear within.
Even just the wiggle of a finger
Would give them hope to win.

Sitting hopelessly in the hands of fate,
They can but take the ride
And step into whatever unfold
Until they end their lives.

Then suddenly in the very next instance,
The events of everything change.
'Tis like a dreamland of nightmares,
Controlled by claws and fangs,

Where all perception is haggardly slowed
Into nonsensible patterns.
This is unreal; forget reality
And what it's telling them.

All of this must be an illusion
Even though they don't know how
That three of them simultaneously
Can dream the same outcome.

This mystery now does haunt their minds.
How can the three of them
Dream indeed the exact same dream
Simultaneously?

And add to this the exact same time
With all the same events
Interacting between them all.
Is this coincidence?

Indeed, they doubt it, hoping instead
That this is all a dream.
The problem is how to wake up
And close down the whole scene.

Dracula's voice booms with excitement
And rises a pitch higher
As he has captured the attention
Of all those in the crowd.

"And now unto our honored guests,
Dear Tonie, Tommie, and Ann."
Again his eyes come to a halt
And linger a bit on Ann.
He then proceeds, "We present to them
For the highlight of this evening,
A gift that is their very own,
A must-have before leaving."

Sweeping with a dramatic hand,
He gestures toward the cake,
Then makes the statement loud and bold,
"It's pumpkin surprise today!"

Ice-cold chilling and freezing below,
There are no words to use
Which pierce through the trio's hearts
And now cause them to bruise.

Yea, if indeed there's such a thing
To forge one's worst nightmare
To manifest before one's eyes,
Then for them this comes to bare,

For in the very next same moment
After this announcement,
By everyone, "pumpkin surprise"
Is echoed in unison.

And from that point, all heck breaks loose,
Yea, in the literal sense.
It happens right before their eyes
Before they even blink.
The cake, the giant pumpkin pie,
The top part explodes outward
And spews forth bits of wet debris,
Like a hot volcano's mouth.

Indeed, as startling as this may be,
This isn't the discomfort
That causes their bones to now unhinge
And go weak in the joints.

But rather, it is who they see
Than what have just now happened,
For bursting from the cake they see
Him, the headless horseman.

Déjà vu, it's happening again,
Their very archvillain returns
Whose cry of vengeance in their heads
Is like a torch that burns.

He sails the air upon his steed,
Sending hot, hurtful thoughts
Of the sweet revenge that this will be
With all the time he's got.

Time and circumstance have changed,
No flimsy pumpkin head;
But now he sports a glistening sword,
Which glows like red-hot lead.
Their reflection bounces from his sword
To show their pitiful state,
Tied and trestle, a gift-wrapped package
Now served forth as a steak.

There's nothing better that he can ask
Than what he now has here.
A payback joyous as sweet as pie,
This from his mind they hear.

He seems to have a sentiment,
A specialty for the girl,
With jet-black hair and petty eyes
Whose skin's now white as pearls.

They mutter in unison under their breath,
"In the name of our dear Lord."
It's not a swear but sincere prayer,
Seeking help from up above.

This is because of where they are.
They're in a world unknown,
Far out from what they ever imagined,
Yea, far beyond the norm.

Their eyes show that they have seen death
And now know its decree.
Beyond the horror and shock, they're shaken
With this eternity.
Their guillotine execution,
It is but the beginning.
They see this plainly without a doubt
And know that they should scream.

And if they did, unto what purpose?
What help would it now bring?
'Twould only be wasted energy
Amid their enemies.

So there is nothing they can do,
And this is evident.
So at this point, they will not waste
Their moves on senselessness.

THE TRIO'S DEMISE

The headless horseman has the glory,
Victory is in his hand.
With his muscled arm, he swings his sword,
Which responds to his command.

The swing is clean; there's no resistance,
Slicing through bones and flesh.
Connecting with its sought out victims,
The hens brought home to nest.

The bodies of Tonie and Ann and Tommie
Resist not the assault,
But cordially they do comply
And do not call a halt.

There's no resistance on their part,
Being trampled underfoot
As the onslaught permeates the room,
Spewing cracked and splintered wood.

The speed is awesome, defying the eyes
Thus giving invisibility
Unto the demise of what once was
Giving their souls true liberty.

The straps are gone which held them tight.
There's no more need for them.
The bodies are gone where once did sat
The famous trio victims.

The chairs are mangled in a lifeless heap.
There's nothing left to see.
The headless horseman did the job
In bringing the victory.

Thunderous cheers and roaring rumblings
Do echo the great big hall.
It is so powerful the building's foundation
Is rocking from it all.

With this happening, it takes a moment
To filter in the sound
Of slamming doors and clicking locks
That turn everything around.

A hush-hush silence fills the chamber,
And time itself has stopped
As things unfold before their eyes,
Which brings them to a halt.

The headless horseman, Dracula,
And all the other hordes
Now see the scene for what it is
And tread it all the more.
For there among the mangled pile,
There are no bodies found.
The three heads of decapitation
Are neither on the ground.

Not a single sign is left at all
Of Tonie, Tommie, and Ann.
It seems that they have gotten away
And vanished once again.

THE TRIO'S RESURRECTION

Now once again, the ruckus starts
With this new realization
But not with sounds of good, glad tidings,
Rather hostile demonstrations.

To say they're mad is understated.
They're livid as can be,
And what goes on behind those doors,
The trio don't want to see.

Nor do they wait to find out what
Locked doors are keeping back.
An old expression wise and true
Now put them back on track.

Look not a gift horse in the mouth,
And that is what they're doing.
They're heading home with no more stops,
And this they will not ruin.

They race with speed through the empty building,
Outrunning their own echoes.
As now convinced that everyone else
Was at the ceremony hole.

Whether or not it doesn't matter,
With urgency do they move.
Unprecedented in their speed,
They keep a steady groove.

Through winding passages, doors, and stairs,
And all the other obstacles,
They keep on moving and will not stop
Lest they melt like popsicles.

Whatever does be the unseen force
That's driving them at will,
They do obey obediently
Because they want to live.

Their hearts are pounding, their faces flushed.
Their limbs are taunt and tight.
Their hairs are bristling on their bodies
With static electric fire.

In spite of this, they aren't detoured
And will not halt their stride.
But giving their freedom complete attention,
Everything is put in flight.

They see the front door finally,
The entrance plain in view.
It's here that they, for the briefest moment,
Recall this last rescue.
Now, this is what they do recall
When they were in the chamber,
Hog-tied and bound with no rescue,
No tools, no saw, no hammer.

They lacked all means of any escape,
And hope was gone as well.
But still they prayed against all hope.
Somehow faith would prevail.

Then suddenly out of nowhere
From their deepest inner parts,
At their bleakest moment of life
Erupted a fiery spark.

A surge of energy bolted through them
Like nothing they can recall.
All consuming and uninhibited,
It settled upon them all.

And everything that were about them
Seemed only as an illusion,
And all else faltered in their presence
As they found themselves a moving.

The only thing printed on their minds,
'Twas to run just like the wind,
And they indeed by God obeyed
And made their way toward freedom.

Finally Home

And now that very same proposition
Is set before them now;
And they will take it, yes, indeed,
As heaven so allow.

And so it is without delay,
They head for the front door.
All grasp the knob at the same time,
Then through the door they pour.

Outside the house into warm air
But cold unto their skin,
They hit the ground not breaking speed,
Trying to catch the wind.

And looking up into the sky,
They see the bright stars shining,
Which overwash them with all joy
Despite the weather's discomfort.

This is topped off by sweet relief,
Looking up into the heaven
And sighting a shooting comet pass by
In their opposite heading direction.

There's a strong temptation to look back,
Overwhelming with desire,
But they're determined and know what's better.
It's not worth losing their lives.

And so they fortify themselves
And push themselves on through
Till very soon things are familiar
That comes into their view.

Yea, even though they do slow down,
It's to a lively trot,
Which cools them down a little bit
From being oh so hot.

And then it is with so much joy
That they take in the sight
The wooden bridge that leads them back
To the church with the bright light.

It still shines bright with a luminous glow,
The same one from before
Of which they had not taken note,
But now they give it focus.

They give one another a knowing look.
There are no spoken words.
Then crossing the bridge uneventfully,
The best news they've been served.
And when they reach the other side
And their feet leave the bridge,
Yea, all oppressive vibes and whelms
Are immediately dismissed.

Until this point, they had not known
What crushing weight they bore,
But now they simultaneously
Sigh with relief of joy.

About the Author

Thomas Laidler was born in Orlando, Florida, where he graduated from Evans High School where he enlisted into the US Navy six months before his graduation. Upon his enlistment into the service, he was assigned to Selfridge Air National Guard Base as an aviation electrical technician assigned in the homeland to the task of training and preparing active reserves for combat readiness after attending various high-level technical classes and courses, as well as instructor classes.

He served six years with an honorable discharge. Upon discharge, he was hired into the USPS and has been currently working there for the last thirty-five years. He married a year after his postal job and had two children, a boy and a girl. Shortly after his discharge, he began an ordained deacon then a minister at his local church, where he faithfully serves his community. His interests and hobbies are writing, music, and art or drawing. He has various poems published in the Best Poet Editions of 2017 and 2018. His desire and wish is to inspire, encourage, and enlighten as many as possible toward a positive, productive, and healthy perspective on the outlook of life to always have hope via his words of inspiration.

www.ingramcontent.com/pod-product-compliance
Lightning Source LLC
Chambersburg PA
CBHW040907010826
48978CB00013BB/1182